THE GOOD MOTHER

A GRIPPING PSYCHOLOGICAL THRILLER

ALAN PETERSEN

17th
Street
B O O K S

JOIN ME

Want to be the first to get exclusive insights into my books, hear the latest news, and enjoy sneak peeks and more? Join my newsletter!

It's easy! Just sign up at www.alanpetersen.com/signup

PROLOGUE

THE LAST TIME HE TOUCHED ME, I MADE A VOW: never again.

He'd first come into my room not long after I was placed under his care. That was six months ago, maybe. I try not to think about the past, or time, much.

I couldn't seem to get his smell off my body. I took a Karen Silkwood shower after. But no matter how hot the water or how hard I scrubbed, I could never wash his stench from my skin.

His smell clung to me long after he left the room. Sometimes I was certain other people could smell it too, so I wrapped myself in oversized hoodies and sweatpants and tried to disappear into the fabric. Kids teased me about it at school, but I didn't care.

It felt safer to hide my body—especially my wrists. I

kept the sleeve pulled down over the mark there, a thin reminder of the moment things had gotten too dark. Covering it didn't erase anything, but it made me feel like I could disappear from the eyes that always seemed to find me.

Even on nights when he didn't sneak into my room, he lived in my head. The dreams were so vivid I could feel his weight pressing down on me, smell the beer and cigarettes on his breath, the grit of his stubble against my cheek. I'd lie awake in short bursts of sleep; minutes, an hour. Then the nightmare would start again.

On those nights, when he did come into my room, he climbed on top of me without a word. I closed my eyes and waited for it to be over. The only relief was the sound of the mattress settling when he left, the sound of my door closing, and the creak of the floorboards up the hall. That was the man the foster system had trusted to keep me safe.

I hated him. I hated the system that had dropped me into his house with a *job done* shrug. This was my third placement since my parents had died. The first two were cold and mean, but at least they hadn't taken my body like he had. Too many times to count.

His wife, my foster mother, pretended not to know—but that was bullshit. She knew what was going on. I even tried to tell her once, and she backhanded me and called me a liar. After that, she looked at me with disgust, as if I'd seduced her husband, as if I were the threat. A character in a Nabokov novel.

She had made it clear what I meant to her: "You're just a paycheck," she said once. I hated her almost as much as I hated him.

Those nights began the same. A messed-up ritual. He always paced outside my door first. It was a rhythm I'd learned to predict. The pitter-patter of his feet behind my closed door. It was as if he was psyching himself into entering my room. Maybe he felt guilty. Whatever he did out there, it wasn't enough for him to walk away and leave me alone.

I didn't need to know what went through his head. I only needed to know what I would do about it.

Tonight, when the knob turned and the door creaked open, I was ready to keep my promise.

I had wrapped my fingers around the shotgun hours earlier and slid it under the bed. He kept guns and ammunition in the basement, unlocked. He didn't seem concerned about gun safety. He should have been.

I didn't know much about guns, but this one had *Mossberg* etched into the barrel. So I entered it into the search box and watched videos online that showed me the basics.

When I was alone in the house, I practiced loading and racking it just like in the videos I had watched.

It seemed simple. I was going to find out soon enough.

He followed the same slow, practiced rhythm he always did. He didn't say anything as he approached my bed. But this time, I didn't pretend to be asleep. I pulled the blanket aside, took the gun in both hands, and aimed.

When he saw the barrel, the look on his face gave me a power I'd never felt. Before he could move, before he could scream or run, I pulled the trigger.

It was louder than I thought it would be. The kick hit my shoulder and pain bloomed, hot and immediate. What they didn't talk about in those videos was the blood. There was so much blood, and it splattered across my face like I was in a horror movie. I should have been shaking. I should have been sobbing. I should have felt nauseous. I felt none of it.

When the shouting started in the house, I aimed at the door and waited. If she came in, I would do it again. Instead, I heard the front door opening and heard her screams outside.

Through the window, I saw her stumble across the yard, screaming. Turned out she wasn't as passed out as she pretended to be.

I put the shotgun down and waited.

Waiting felt strange. It was quiet in a way I had never known. The clock in the hallway ticked loudly enough to be a drum. The taste of copper filled my mouth where the blood had spat on my lips; the warm blood now felt cold. I wiped at it with the back of my hand like it was nothing. I thought of running, of throwing the gun in the bushes and walking away—maybe hitchhiking to nowhere. But I knew that was a fantasy. The cops would find me. I had no money even to run down to the corner store and buy a soda. You needed money to get away with crimes like this. To start a new life, somewhere tropical. More fantasy.

I looked at his lifeless body. His face looked like a raw hamburger. I felt no guilt. The thought of him still breathing in this world, of him finding some other child and doing the same thing, made my hands go cold again. There was an ugly, steady logic to what I had done. It felt like removing a splinter that had been buried in my skin for years.

Neighbors came out shouting. Someone yelled, "Dial 911."

It didn't take long. I listened to shoes on the pavement and the far wailing of sirens that kept getting louder. I could hear my own breathing and it sounded calm, too calm.

I looked around my room, knowing I would never see it again. And that was fine with me.

The police came. I moved from the foster care system into the penal system. People asked questions, used words like *tragedy* and *system failures*. How could a child feel this was her only option? If the so-called experts couldn't agree on what had happened, and why I did what I did, how could I?

I waited for the flood of guilt that never came. No tears, no remorse, no shaking hands. Instead, for the first time in my life, I felt control.

And I liked it.

ONE

SCHOOL DROP-OFF IN MARIN COUNTY WAS A FULL-contact sport of passive aggression. Teslas and Porsche SUVs idled in a ballet of entitlement, noses angled two feet into the crosswalk like stakes claiming territory. Moms in identical black athleisure and white sneakers power-walked with oat-milk lattes and monogrammed Hydro Flasks, phones on speaker: "Pilates at nine, facial at ten, can you take Kendall to piano lesson?" Yoga mats lay rolled in backseats ready for action. Nannies chatted in Spanish as they pushed Bugaboos with fair-haired toddlers while a dad in a Patagonia vest checked his phone and pretended not to block the fire lane.

The private-school banner fluttered above a curb painted red "for safety," which mostly meant for other people. A volunteer in a safety vest waved like a stressed-out air-traffic controller; no one looked at him. A woman in a quilted jacket mouthed, "Are you *kidding*?" as another car slid into the last legal spot with the grace of a docking yacht. Someone's Golden Retriever wore a bandana for spirit week. Someone else whispered about the gala auction lot—four nights in Cabo, starting bid at five figures —and whether the head-of-school's wife had jumped the kindergarten waitlist for a friend's kid.

At the curb, kisses were quick, backpacks impossibly small for the price of tuition. "Remember—mindfulness!" one mom called, then laid on the horn at an Audi Q6 E-tron that hesitated. A pair of PTA board moms—fundraising royalty—stood sentry with clipboards, collecting volunteers like tithes. The smell of eucalyptus and espresso hung over the whole performance, clean and sharp.

Tuesdays, after I dropped Lucy, I let the parade finish swallowing itself. Then I cut across to downtown Vista Bay to meet Madison Taylor for brunch—our ritual debrief on all the little wars no one would admit were happening.

Vista Bay was an affluent community in Marin County, perched just across the Golden Gate Bridge from San Francisco on the Tiburon Peninsula. It offered water-front vistas, manicured streets, and small-town charm with the wealth of a small nation.

The brunch was a welcome distraction. Not just from the school drop off, but from my own troubles at home. French scrambled eggs and mimosas at a café off Main

Street. Madison could talk for hours about Pilates instructors and her son's violin recitals. Normal things. Safe things. The kind of conversation that reminded me of the life I was supposed to be living—a picture-perfect wife, mother, family.

But lately, the picture was starting to crack. During the last few brunches I'd started to confide in Madison about my marriage. Never about my childhood—no one knew that—but I had admitted I was worried about Braden. How distant he'd become.

I wasn't sure why I'd opened up. Madison and I were friendly mostly through our kids and proximity. The truth was, I didn't have many friends. And aside from Braden and Lucy, I had no real family to speak of — an oddity in this upscale world I live in now. My background was nothing like the women here.

Sometimes it feels like my past belongs to someone else entirely.

If the housewives of Marin County knew the truth about where I came from, what I had done as a teenager, they'd gossip me into exile. Sometimes I imagined them putting me on a raft, shoving me out into the bay, and pushing me toward the Pacific where I belonged.

I'd never really fit in, though I had married into one of the most revered old-money families in San Francisco—the Morrisseys. At first, I wore that last name like a badge of honor. But the reality was lonely. So when Madison and I clicked, I latched onto her friendship like a drowning person clutching a life ring.

Madison overshared about everything: seventy vacation photos dumped into a single Facebook post, Instagrammed meals, even her sex life with Jason. At first her candor made me anxious, but soon it felt good to talk to someone. To let out some of what I'd been carrying, even if it was only a fraction of the truth.

Our conversations about kids and yoga soon tilted into something else.

"Jenna," Madison said, lowering her Gucci sunglasses to the tabletop as if bracing for impact, "how are things with Braden? Is he still acting weird?"

I laughed nervously. Too fast. Too brittle. "He is. When I ask him about it, he just says it's work stuff. A big M&A deal he's been working on, and it's not going well."

"That makes sense, honey. Jason gets unbearable when things are going bad at work. Maybe Braden's the same way."

It was true; our husbands were cut from the same cloth. Jason's fortune came from East Coast steel, Braden's from West Coast lumber. Yale and Stanford. Different pedigrees, same dynasties. As a high-powered attorney, stress came with the territory. But this felt different. Braden wasn't just stressed, he was drifting away. Shutting me out.

"He hasn't touched me in three months," I blurted. Heat crawled up my cheeks.

Madison's eyes widened, but only for a beat. Then she leaned in, whispering, "Really? That long?"

I nodded, staring at my creamy eggs, holding back tears. I wasn't going to cry in a café. Not here.

"Have you tried making the first move? Sometimes I have to tell Jason flat out: *If you don't take me to bed tonight, I'm going to lose it.*"

That made me chuckle, despite myself. "I've made it clear. He just rejects me. Says he's too stressed. That can't be a good sign."

"Well..." Madison hesitated, clearly searching for a comforting explanation and coming up empty.

"If he's not getting it from me, then he's getting it somewhere else, right?"

"No. Not necessarily," she said. "Don't let those thoughts eat you alive."

I wanted to believe her. But it was easier said than done.

THAT EVENING, I had dinner ready. The ferry schedule said Braden should've been home by six, but that time came and went. I was about to text him when my phone buzzed first:

Swamped at work. Don't wait up. I'll eat at the office.

So Lucy and I ate spaghetti and meatballs at the kitchen island. She made me laugh telling a story about a spelling bee and her teacher's crooked tie. Later, I tucked her into bed, kissed her forehead, and lingered too long in her doorway. She was the one part of my life that still felt safe.

By the time I slipped into my own room, the house was quiet. I propped myself up with pillows, a book in hand, though the words blurred together. Madison's voice replayed in my head. *Is he still acting weird?*

I told myself he'd crawl into bed beside me any minute, that we'd make love, that tomorrow everything would feel normal again. I almost convinced myself.

Then the garage door rumbled open.

The thump of his shoes in the kitchen. The clink of glass. Ice in a tumbler. Bourbon. I knew the sounds too well.

A pause. Then the soft sliding of the patio door.

I held still, listening, debating whether to go down. Finally, I slipped out of bed and padded to the landing.

He was on the second-floor deck, wrapped in the chill drifting off the bay—a glass of bourbon in his hand, the bottle and an ice bucket on the table beside him. The Golden Gate Bridge shimmered beyond, its towers glowing in yellow light, fog curling low across the water.

Braden didn't turn when I stepped outside. He just stared at the bridge, swirling his glass.

"Sorry, I didn't want to wake you," he said somberly.

"What's wrong?" I asked, my tone careful.

He shrugged. "Just had another bad day at work."

That was all. No further explanation, just an awkward silence. I wrapped my arms around myself against the cold, waiting for more. He gave me nothing.

Then his phone lit up on the table between us, a small square of light cutting through the dark. I couldn't help but glance down.

Heather — We need to talk.

I felt lightheaded.

Braden's hand moved fast, snapping the screen dark. He didn't look at me. Didn't offer an explanation.

I waited for him to say something—anything—but he kept his eyes fixed on the bay, swirling the bourbon in his glass.

Finally he lifted it, took a slow sip, and said, "You don't have to wait up for me."

Dismissed.

I stood there longer than I should have, studying the slope of his shoulders, the rigid set of his jaw. Then I turned, went back inside, and closed the door.

TWO

THE NEXT MORNING I WOKE EARLY BUT NOT RESTED. I'd spent half the night listening for Braden to come inside, waiting for the soft dip of the mattress that never happened. When sleep finally came, it was shallow and restless, and when I opened my eyes, the fog outside the window was thick and Braden's side of the bed empty.

Lucy was already awake, humming to herself as she got dressed for school. Her small routines were my anchor. Pack her lunch. Remind her to brush her teeth. I tried to smooth her hair into a braid, but she gave me the classic "It's fine, Mom" wave-off. A preview of the coming tween and teenage years.

She was still young enough to reach back for my hand as we crossed the school parking lot, though. I held on longer than I should have, savoring the warmth of her palm before she pulled away, already caught up in the world of her friends waiting at the gate.

Braden had left at six-thirty in the morning to catch the first ferry to San Francisco from Tiburon. We spoke maybe fifty words to each other from the time he got home until he left again. Just logistics. Lucy's soccer schedule, the dry cleaning, what he wanted for dinner. Nothing real. Nothing of substance.

The house felt too quiet after I dropped Lucy at school. Her chatter always lingered in the car, but by the time I pulled into the driveway, I was met with utter silence.

I tried to fill it with music, the old Fleetwood Mac playlist Braden once claimed he loved, though lately he only listened to podcasts about finance and litigation. I folded laundry in the bedroom, the lyrics bleeding into the walls, but my mind kept circling back to the text I'd seen the night before.

Heather. *We need to talk.*

The only Heather I knew was his paralegal. So the message had to be something benign, something work-related. But the words clung to me like a burr I couldn't pull free. *We need to talk* sounded personal. And why would she text him at ten at night? The message replayed each time I closed my eyes. Was that why he rejected me? Heather was satisfying his needs. I shook the image from my head, ashamed of how vividly I could picture it.

By mid-morning, I found myself wandering into Braden's home office. I wasn't snooping, not really. I only needed the water bill from the printer. At least, that's what I told myself.

The office smelled faintly of his cologne—sandalwood and something sharper, the same scent I used to press my face against in bed. Was Heather doing that now?

His desk was cluttered with files, gold cufflinks, and a stack of unopened mail. The blinds were tilted open just enough for a bar of light to cut across the desk. And there, glowing on the monitor, was his work email. Logged in. Wide open.

I froze.

I knew better. I wasn't supposed to look. His inbox wasn't mine. We had an unspoken rule about boundaries, though lately he'd been rewriting the rules without telling me.

Before I could retreat, before I could pretend I hadn't seen, a new message pinged at the top of the screen.

From: **Heather Evans**

Subject: **HR can't ignore this**

My knees buckled.

The preview text showed just enough to lodge in my throat: *I told you this would happen if ...*

And then, in an instant, it vanished.

The line blinked away. The message was gone, as if it had never existed. I clicked desperately, heart hammering, but the inbox refreshed to nothing. He'd deleted it remotely. Or maybe some setting wiped it clean. I didn't know.

The silence of the office deepened around me, pressing in. I could almost hear my pulse echoing against the glass of framed diplomas from Stanford on the wall. A pedigree that made Braden untouchable in most rooms. Now all I saw were cracks in the frame.

I shut down the screen as every nerve in my body seemed to surge from head to toe. I walked out like the room might explode if I stayed a second longer.

The rest of the day was a blur. I pushed a cart through the grocery store aisles without remembering what I'd bought. I skipped my therapy appointment because I couldn't imagine putting words to the chaos in my head. Even answering routine questions—"How have you been sleeping?"—felt impossible when I wasn't sure I could trust my own perception anymore.

By dinner, Braden was home, sleeves rolled, hair mussed from what looked like a long day. Lucy chatted beside him about a science experiment gone wrong, and he laughed in all the right places. He looked like himself. Like the man everyone thought he was.

But I watched his eyes. The way they slid past me too quickly. The way he reached for the wine without asking if I wanted more. It was all so practiced, so normal, it felt staged.

I smiled too tightly, poured myself another glass, and nodded at the right moments. But the text message and the email subject line burned across my mind: *We need to talk. HR can't ignore this.*

Lying in bed that night, with Braden breathing evenly beside me, I stared into the dark, wide awake.

He was having an affair with Heather, my head said. I'd met her once, briefly, at a firm event. She was young, pretty. Brunette, like me. I suppose Braden had a type. The sense of betrayal felt like a chokehold. But if these were messages between lovers, what was the veiled threat about HR?

Could he have done something inappropriate toward her at work? Braden had always been a gentleman. Never once, when we were dating or married, did he try to force me into anything I wasn't willing to do. And he loved his job too much to risk it all on a reckless mistake with his paralegal—a woman at least twenty years younger than him.

It didn't make sense.

I should have woken him. Demanded answers. We needed to talk too, no matter the hour. But I didn't.

There I lay, a coward, staring into the dark, the silence between us louder than any confession he could have made.

THREE

I was up earlier than usual the next morning. After hours of tossing and turning, I finally gave up on sleep around 5:30 and slipped out of bed.

Braden stirred, cracked one eye open. "You're getting up?" His voice was raspy, thick with sleep.

"I can't sleep. I'm going for a run."

"Okay," he murmured, already fading again. Whether from exhaustion, stress, or the bourbon, I couldn't tell.

Halfway down the stairs, I spotted the bottle on the counter—half empty, the crystal glass beside it with a thin amber ring clinging to the bottom. That answered the question.

Outside, the air bit at my skin. I stretched on the porch, my breath fogging in the cold. Dew clung to the railing, the boards slick beneath my running shoes. I set off down the long steep driveway toward the road. The bay was still half-asleep beneath a veil of fog, gulls cutting pale shapes across the gray.

A coyote darted across the street ahead of me, vanishing into the woods. Their presence had become common in recent years, yet seeing one still sent a pulse through me. It moved with purpose; nervous, alert, surviving on the edge of comfort. I understood that feeling. Maybe that's why I couldn't stop watching it disappear into the trees. It was also why we kept a careful eye on our Cavalier, Sunny, when he was in the backyard doing his business.

My therapist says trauma rearranges memory, but running always felt like the only thing that put mine in order. Three miles today. Long enough to loosen the tightness in my chest, but not long enough to keep my thoughts from spiraling.

The road wound along the hillside between manicured hedges and Mediterranean-style mansions clinging to the cliff's edge. Most windows were still dark; only the sound of my shoes on asphalt and the rhythm of my breath kept me company.

I ran past houses I knew only by the shapes of their gates, by the scent of jasmine or eucalyptus drifting through their driveways. Each house looked immaculate, curated—perfect. I wondered how many of the couples inside were like us: beautiful façades hiding hairline cracks. Maybe we were all pretending in this neighborhood. Pretending was practically a sport here.

By the time I reached the house with the purple gate—what Lucy and I jokingly called the Prince House—I turned back toward home. The fog had started to lift, revealing the faint shimmer of the bridge. Somewhere in the distance, the low wail of a foghorn echoed across the water, long and mournful.

Twenty-four minutes later, I reached our driveway, sweat cooling against my skin. The smell of coffee drifted through the open kitchen window—a sign Braden was awake. I paused on the porch for a moment, catching my breath, reluctant to step back inside.

Upstairs, I found him knotting his tie, the picture of composure.

"How was the run?" he asked, sounding disarmingly normal. I was always amazed how quickly he could go from dead sleep to heading out the door dressed to the nines.

"Good. I needed it," I said, grabbing a towel.

"Jenna..." He paused, meeting my eyes in the mirror. "I'm sorry for being such an asshole these past couple months."

The words caught me off guard.

"I just—" He sighed, shoulders sagging. "Work's a mess. Documents went missing, deadlines are slipping. It's the first time I've really screwed up, and I don't know how to handle it. When I get home, I shut down. That's not fair to you. I know that now."

My throat tightened. "Thank you for saying that. It hurts, Braden. You're shutting me out, and I don't know what to think."

"I'll fill you in tonight, I promise. But I have to catch that ferry." He checked his watch, already shifting back into motion.

As frustrating as it was, I nodded. At least he'd admitted something was wrong. Maybe there really was a crisis at work. Maybe all the secrecy and tension was about that—nothing more.

"I'll make dinner," I said. "We'll talk tonight."

He gave me a kiss, brief but real—the first in weeks. My knees went weak with the sudden rush of familiarity.

He spent a few minutes with Lucy, who had just woken up and was still rubbing sleep from her eyes, then grabbed his briefcase and was gone. The sound of the garage door closing echoed through the house. I watched from the window as he drove down the steep driveway toward the park-and-ride lot in Tiburon, where commuters left their cars before catching the early boat to San Francisco.

A few minutes later, faint through the thinning fog, I heard the foghorn again. For a moment, I pictured him on the ferry—his coat collar turned up, to-go cup of coffee in hand, staring at the skyline like any other overworked suburbanite heading into the city.

I made it down to the kitchen, staring at the cooling coffee in his mug. Relief slid through me—thin, temporary, like steam rising and disappearing. I dumped the coffee out, rinsed the cup, and poured myself a fresh one. The bitterness tasted sharper than usual, but I welcomed the caffeine kick.

Outside, Lucy was letting Sunny into the yard. I heard the soft jingle of his collar, and her sleepy voice coaxing him to hurry.

"Keep an eye on Sunny, Luce," I called. "I saw a coyote down the road just now."

"Okay, Mom."

Her voice floated in from the patio door—carefree, trusting. I wished I could borrow some of that.

I sat at the kitchen island, elbows on the counter, staring into my coffee. Thinking about what Braden had said.

Maybe he truly was overwhelmed. Maybe Heather was just part of the chaos at the firm. But even as I tried to believe it, the image of her name on his phone burned behind my eyes like a warning light I couldn't switch off.

After telling Lucy to get ready for school, I stepped into the shower, letting the hot water beat against my skin until I almost convinced myself everything was fine.

Almost.

But that was wishful thinking. No matter how hard I tried to get Braden to let me in, something told me the truth wouldn't make me feel better. He said we'd talk tonight, but what if that conversation was the end of us? What if I was about to be replaced by the younger, prettier Heather Evans?

FOUR

THE FERRY'S DECK VIBRATED SOFTLY BENEATH MY leather Ferragamo Oxford shoes. The engines thrummed as it trudged down the Raccoon Strait towards a thick wall of fog that partially hid the city behind it. I stood at the railing, bad ferry coffee in hand, watching the city skyline appear through the mist.

For the first time in weeks, I felt lighter. I'd actually talked to Jenna this morning. Not the full truth, but enough to ease the tension that had been strangling us both. She didn't have an inkling of what I'd really been dealing with, and that was for the best. The less she knew, the safer she would be. I told myself that, anyway. But who was I kidding? I was protecting myself.

And that wall of silence I had put up chipped away at us, one lie at a time. Now it seemed things had spiraled so badly out of control that it might be too late to come clean.

I could still see her face when I'd told her I was sorry. The way her shoulders dropped, just slightly, like she'd been waiting months to hear those words. I'd meant it, every one of them.

The fog had swallowed Alcatraz to my right. I took a sip of lukewarm coffee and leaned my elbows on the cold railing. The engine's quiet thrum mixed with muffled sounds of conversations drifting around me. Suits and briefcases. People checking their phones, scanning emails, furiously tapping into laptops, doom scrolling. I blended right in with the herd.

I adjusted the strap of my TUMI bag, slung across my shoulder, the one Jenna had given me last Christmas. My initials—BAM—were embossed on the leather tag. Jenna had laughed when she'd first noticed. "BAM! Like a comic book sound effect," she'd said, snapping her fingers. It became a private joke between us.

Now the sight of those letters made my stomach tighten.

I wasn't the same man who'd earned them.

When the ferry docked, I shuffled off with the crowd, my shoes clicking against the metal gangway leading to the pier, a gull perched on a piling watching the whole procession. The air smelled of salt and diesel and roasted coffee from the kiosk nearby. I joined the line of office-bound commuters flowing along the Embarcadero, all of us moving on autopilot towards our office jobs.

My phone pinged in my jacket pocket. I ignored it. I already knew it wasn't good news.

Turning onto Market, I merged with the river of people heading toward the Financial District. The crowd of office dwellers still hadn't fully recovered from the lockdowns, but it was getting busier, which was good news for the City.

The glass towers rose ahead, cold and gleaming. I veered right on Montgomery Street, where my building loomed above me like a gray monolith—twenty-seven floors of ambition and quiet desperation.

I'd always liked the place; it was a monument to a bygone era. The building, constructed in the late 1980s, paid homage to the Art Deco skyscrapers of the 1930s. It blended modern aesthetics with a nostalgic feel, recalling a time when men wore hats, enjoyed Martini lunches, and offices had secretarial pools that covered an entire floor.

Funny how a building could fool you like that.

The elevator ride up felt longer than usual. A few faces were familiar, but no one spoke. Most were sealed inside their own private worlds by white pods tucked in their ears. Everyone minded their own business, eyes fixed on the glowing floor numbers, ready to sprint like thoroughbreds out the gate. The silence was polite, professional. A version of civility.

On the twentieth floor, the firm's logo—black letters etched in steel—greeted me like a judgment.

Langford, Hayes & Fox LLP.

I walked through the glass doors into the open lobby. Paige, the receptionist, gave me a small sympathetic smile that set off alarm bells in my head.

"Morning, Braden," she said quietly.

I nodded. "Morning."

As I moved past reception, I could feel eyes flicking toward me, then away. The merger was collapsing, and everyone knew it. I was the lead partner on the deal, which made me a dead man walking. No one wanted to catch whatever professional contagion I was carrying.

Months of work. Endless negotiations. Then one mishap after another, until the client's patience finally snapped. Confidential documents were sent to the wrong address, others had gone missing, and the blame now circled toward me.

I'd told myself I could fix it before anyone noticed. But it seemed everyone already had.

The walk to my office felt longer than it should have. When I stepped inside, the first thing I saw was the red light blinking on my phone. Two new voicemails. And on my monitor, an unread email.

Client: Hudson Therapeutics.

Subject: Failure to Meet Service-Level Agreement.

I closed my eyes and exhaled slowly. So that was that. The merger was dead. Missing the SLA gave them all the ammunition they needed to fire the firm. Instead of collecting a hefty fee at closing, the firm would now owe a hefty fine for not hitting the SLA. I was fucked.

My stomach turned. The word *failure* loomed on the screen, and that's exactly how I felt—like a failure.

I slumped into my chair and stared at the screen, then let my gaze drift to the window. I couldn't remember the last time I'd just looked out. Montgomery Street cut between the FiDi towers, angling toward Telegraph Hill, where multimillion-dollar homes were stacked up the slope.

My phone trilled again. Another email notification popped up.

From: HR Department

Subject: Confidential: Complaint Filed — Immediate Response Required

The timing couldn't be worse. When it rains, it pours, I supposed.

For a moment, I didn't move. My throat went dry.

I clicked it open, heart thudding.

Braden,

A formal complaint has been filed regarding inappropriate conduct toward a subordinate.

The rest of the email became blurry.

Heather.

She had followed through on her threat.

Heather had been playing these head games with me for the past month. Although she had threatened to do something like this, I'd never thought she would go through with it, since she professed to have feelings for me. I thought I could handle her; how could I have been so wrong?

I pressed my fingers to my temples. The bourbon from last night still pulsed behind my eyes.

The office door creaked open. Timothy Peck, a managing partner, mentor, and now executioner, stood there in his immaculate navy suit. He didn't bother with small talk.

"Conference room, Braden. Now."

Like obedient cattle being led to the slaughter, I followed him down the hall. I walked past glass offices that might as well have been fishtanks as people watched, whispering, pretending not to. I was the car wreck you see on the side of the road that you can't stop gawking at.

The conference room was cold and the HVAC suddenly seemed too loud. Two HR reps sat across from Peck's chair, laptops open. One of them, a woman named Alexis, offered a strained smile.

"Braden," she said, gesturing to the seat across from her. "Please sit."

I did.

Peck folded his hands, the picture of restrained fury. "You know why you're here?"

I'm an attorney. I know I should keep my mouth shut

when being questioned by police or by my employer. But I couldn't.

"I assume this is about Heather Evans." I sounded steadier than I felt.

No one confirmed that, they just leaned back, accusatory eyes on me. Peck broke the silence. "The client terminated the firm over the failed merger you led. And now this complaint lands on my desk. All in one day. The optics couldn't be any worse for you, Braden. Very bad."

"I didn't do anything," I said. "This is retaliation. She's angry because I—"

Alexis raised a hand, calm but firm. "We're not here to debate intent. The firm has a zero-tolerance policy towards sexual harassment. You've been terminated effective immediately."

Although I knew it was coming, the words hit harder than I expected. Heather had followed through with her threats.

I'd braced for a hit over the blown merger, but I couldn't fathom that they'd fire me. Not like this. *At least allow me a graceful exit, a mutual separation. Give me a couple months to land at another firm.* Instead, I was taking a double gut punch: the biggest deal of my career imploding and a sexual harassment complaint, all before nine a.m.

I looked at my mentor hoping for mercy, but Peck looked away. "Turn in your keycard and firm-issued laptop.

Security will escort you out. HR will follow up regarding your personal items."

It was over. Just like that. I couldn't even go to my office to pack up my things.

I wanted to fight, to argue, to explain, but the look on everyone in that room told me it wouldn't matter. The decision had already been made somewhere far above.

When I left the conference room, a security guard in a blue polyester blazer holding a black two-way radio was waiting. Pleasant but firm, with a don't-make-this-harder-than-it-has-to-be expression. This was humiliating enough already; I wasn't about to make a scene. I just followed him down the hallway and into the elevator.

I could hear a pin drop. The firm's logo on the wall glinted in the light like a blade. My reflection fractured across the chrome doors as we descended.

The guard handed me my bag in the lobby. It felt so light without the laptop in there—a cruel reminder of what was happening.

"The firm will pack up the rest of your personal belongings in your office and FedEx them to your home address."

"Thanks," I said. Why was I thanking him?

He gave me a tight smile and walked away. I stood there alone for a few seconds before finding the gumption to head outside, knowing I would probably never set foot inside this building again.

The city felt colder than usual.

I reached the corner of Montgomery and Market and stopped. The morning crowd streamed past me, oblivious.

For a moment, I just stood there, gripping the strap of my TUMI bag, tracing the worn leather where Jenna's fingers had once run across my initials—BAM.

What was I going to tell her?

Bam. That's what it felt like.

The sound of my life coming apart.

FIVE

I walked down Market Street in a daze, carried by the mid-morning rush like driftwood in a current.

My mind was a hollow echo chamber, replaying the last few hours on a relentless loop: Peck's hard eyes, HR's rehearsed sympathy, the guard's polite escort out of the building. My humiliation was on full display. My things packed and shipped. Put out on the curb like trash waiting for pickup.

And beneath it all, my father's voice: *This sort of thing doesn't happen to a Morrissey.*

Each memory was a fresh stab, and with every step the city, once a vibrant backdrop to my ambitious life, felt more like a stage from which I'd been unceremoniously yanked. My body was on autopilot, a mere vessel propelled by muscle memory, until I finally reached the Ferry Building.

It was barely past ten thirty, an hour that usually

marked the beginning of my most productive calls, not the nadir of my career.

Instead of being a rainmaker on the twentieth floor of a skyscraper, I was on the outside now. Would I be forever, I wondered? Word gets around. By noon, none of the top prestigious firms would want anything to do with me, let alone hire me.

The air here was different, a faint saline tang from the bay mingling with the rich roasted aroma of coffee wafting from the Blue Bottle kiosk.

A handful of joggers, their faces determined, tourists with their wide-eyed wonder, and early commuters already plugged into their daily rhythms dotted the promenade. Soon, I knew, the lunch crowd would descend, transforming this peaceful stretch into a cacophony of chatter and motion. But for now it felt eerily calm, as if the city itself was holding its breath, mirroring the suspended animation of my own existence.

I gravitated toward the weathered wooden benches lining the waterfront, their surfaces worn smooth by countless hands and countless stories.

As I sat, my gaze fixed on the expanse of a bay indifferent to what I was going through.

The ferries, those grand white hulls, carved their paths through the gray-green water, carrying people whose lives still made sense.

I couldn't bring myself to board the ferry. To go home and face Jenna.

I just sat there, watching, frozen. Stunned.

Somewhere further down the promenade, the mournful wail of an electric guitar began to carry on the light breeze. It was a busker, weaving a slow and haunting rendition of "Hotel California" aided by a small, battered Peavey amp. The notes bent and lingered in the air like restless spirits, each chord a heavy sigh. It was the kind of song that twisted the knife, evoking a powerful cocktail of nostalgia for a past that felt irretrievably lost and a suffocating sense of being trapped in the present. I too felt like I could never leave from this darkness that was swallowing me whole.

Across the water, the hills of the Tiburon Peninsula shimmered faintly in the haze, a beacon of home. But the thought of facing Jenna sent a fresh wave of dread through me.

I'd told her we'd talk tonight. She probably thought I meant about stress at work and my being standoffish towards her, not about her husband getting fired and accused of harassment before breakfast. It was something I hadn't seen coming.

The aftermath of the failed merger I could deal with, but how could I tell Jenna about Heather?

How the hell had this happened?

Sure, I'd made mistakes before. Missed a detail, sent a late email. But never this. Never a blown merger under my watch, never the inexplicable disappearance of critical documents.

That wasn't me. That wasn't in my DNA. My father used to say it like gospel: *Morrisseys don't fail.*

But I had. And I had done it spectacularly. The weight of that realization was a crushing burden, pinning me to the bench as I fended off a panic attack. I couldn't get up and board the ferry.

Heather. Her name surfaced in my mind like a venomous serpent, coiling around every thought. It sent me from feeling sorry for myself to a rage towards her that made me fear what I might do if I saw her walking by at this very moment.

Everything, it seemed, had started with her. Six months ago, she had joined my team—bright, undeniably talented, and driven, her ambition wrapped in a seductive veneer of flattery. At first, she had been indispensable, her sharp insights and tireless energy valuable assets.

Then came the awkward flirting. I know people find me attractive, so I'm used to that type of behavior, but not from a subordinate, and not that aggressive. The wedding ring on my finger and the photographs of Jenna and Lucy on my desk didn't seem to dissuade her. But her work was top-notch. When something needed to get done, I trusted her and knew it would get done. Yet, despite her assurances she had sent those documents and filed them on time, seemingly she hadn't.

Now, with the clarity of hindsight, the pattern clicked into place: the strategically missing files, the impeccably timed complaint to HR, the chilling precision of it all.

Had she planned this? The whisper of paranoia grew louder with every passing second. Had she orchestrated my downfall with such meticulous cold-blooded intent?

I reached into my laptop bag, a sudden surge of desperate hope prompting me to dig for my computer, to search for some digital breadcrumb, some irrefutable proof of her machinations. My hand met nothing but air. Right. The laptop, along with my phone, my access badge, and even my office key, had been confiscated the moment I was ushered out; my digital life, my professional identity, had been severed with the clean, brutal efficiency of an executioner's axe.

When I rummaged for my personal phone, it too was missing. I knew the firm wouldn't have taken it. That was strange. It was basically a way for Jenna to get a hold of me at work, and I didn't use it much during the day. I shrugged. I must have left in my car at the ferry parking lot. Gaining time to process everything by being disconnected from the modern world seemed exactly what I needed right now, and I felt relieved.

Hours passed, measured not by the movement of the sun but by the subtle shifts in the air, which turned colder, and in the timbre of the city. The busker's song changed, then that of another, then another, a distant soundtrack to my internal turmoil. The crowd around me thickened, families with cameras capturing moments of joy, couples with their lattes lost in whispered conversations, office workers on their lunch break, their lives unfurling in predictable, reassuring patterns. But I stayed welded to the bench, a ghost among the living, an invisible observer of a world that seemed to have easily moved on without me.

The last ferry to Tiburon was boarding. I couldn't put this off any longer. I stood, legs stiff from sitting for hours, and I joined the short line.

I stepped onto the boat, making my way to the upper deck. The engines roared to life as the boat pulled away from the dock and the city lights shrank behind me.

The wind tore through my hair, whipping strands across my face, and the fine spray from the bay dampened my shirt. I leaned against the cold railing. The water below was a vast, inky black—a shifting, living entity.

It would be so easy.

One step. One slip. A quick, decisive plunge into the cold embrace of the bay. No explaining, no attempting to reconstruct the shattered pieces of my life. No shame, no enduring the pity, or worse, the disgust in Jenna's eyes when she finally understood what had been going on with me. Just silence. A profound, absolute silence that promised an end to the agonizing clamor in my mind.

I closed my eyes. Took a breath.

And leaned in.

SIX

THE AFTERNOON RAN THIN, THE KIND OF DAY THAT refused to end. I tried to write, answer emails, fold laundry —anything to occupy the hours until Braden got home. But my mind kept circling the same loop.

Braden's apology this morning. The promise to talk tonight. The memory of that late-night text from Heather to Braden: *We need to talk.*

By three, the silence in the house had curdled into something heavy. Even Sunny paced near the back door, whining softly, like he sensed it too.

I usually headed out to pick up Lucy from school around this time, but Braden and I needed to talk—really talk—if we were going to repair the fractures in our marriage. And we couldn't do that freely with Lucy at home.

So I called Madison, asking if she could pick up Lucy

along with her son from school. I apologized for the short notice. She didn't hesitate. "Absolutely," she said. Then she laughed. "Besides, I think Chase has a crush on Lucy."

I was halfway through unloading the dishwasher when my phone vibrated on the counter.

It was Greg Boyd, a partner at the firm and one of Braden's closest friends from work. We were on friendly terms, since Braden and I would have dinners with Greg and his wife—but that was the extent of our interactions. He'd never called me directly before. My stomach tightened.

I wiped my hands on a towel and answered. "Hey, Greg."

There was a pause, a sharp intake of breath. "Jenna... I shouldn't be calling. I shouldn't even say this, but—"

He stopped, and I could hear office noise in the background.

"I've been trying to reach Braden, but he's not answering his phone or replying to my text messages."

A cold shiver shot up my spine.

"What do you mean? Isn't he in his office right now?"

Silence.

"I can get in trouble for telling you this," Greg said finally, his voice low. "But I'm worried."

"Greg, please, you're scaring me. Is Braden okay?"

He exhaled. "Braden was... let go."

Let go? The words didn't make sense.

"Are you saying he was fired?"

"Yes. This morning."

The world tilted. "What?"

"I don't know the details. HR's saying it's complicated. But... I'm worried. No one's heard from him since ten, when security walked him out."

This couldn't be true. It must be a horrible prank that Braden had put Greg up to, but I knew neither of them would be so cruel as to do something like that.

Greg interrupted my thoughts: "When was the last time you talked to him?"

"Not since he left for work."

Clearly regretting the call, Greg cleared his throat. "I'm sorry to be the one to tell you, Jenna. I shouldn't have called you."

I couldn't deal with this conversation any longer. I managed something like "thank you" before hanging up. My hands trembled and I leaned against the counter, staring at the neat rows of plates I'd just stacked—as if order could still exist in the face of chaos.

Fired. How can that be?

He'd said the merger was stressful. And that it was going badly, but he hadn't said losing his job was even possible. He was a rainmaker.

My stomach turned. Maybe it wasn't the merger.

Maybe it was *her*. That cryptic message from Heather Evans.

I called him. Straight to voicemail.

His cheerful recorded voice sounded like it came from another era—back when he was happy. When we were happy.

I tried again. Then again. Nothing.

I started texting, my fingers shaking:

Are you okay?

Tried calling.

I know about work.

Please call me.

I'm so worried.

Minutes dragged into hours. By five, I'd lost count of how many times I'd called.

All I could do was send more text messages:

Please let me know you're okay.

Call me or text me.

Just need to know you're okay.

We can get through this.

Come home.

But those text messages were also ignored.

I opened our shared *Find My Phone* account. His location sharing had been turned off.

What the hell was going on?

That was it. I was calling the police. Six hours of waiting was enough.

After being transferred twice and placed on hold for a few minutes, a detective finally picked up.

I told him everything.

"Ma'am, it's too soon to file a missing person report," he said flatly. "He's an adult, recently fired. He's probably blowing off steam at a bar somewhere. It's what I would do. If he's not home by morning, call again."

He practically hung up on me. That was it. No help from law enforcement.

Then the Mercedes app on my phone showed me his car was still at the ferry terminal's park-and-ride lot.

Where the hell was he?

I thought about getting in my car to go look for him. But where? Drive to the city? Or somewhere around Marin County? He could be anywhere. And what if he came home when I was out there, driving around aimlessly to find him. No. I was going to stay put and wait for him here.

He had to come home sooner or later. Right?

I stared at the front door long after the sun went down, waiting for the sound of his key in the lock.

I DON'T KNOW why I thought about making dinner. I wasn't hungry. My mind must have wanted me to do something remotely normal, even an easy recipe like spaghetti marinara to keep me busy. But I couldn't even focus on simple tasks such as boiling water and making sauce.

I sat on the couch in the living room that faced the front door. I spent half an hour staring at it, and at my phone.

Then I heard it. The crunch of tires on the driveway.

Sunny barked once and ran to the door. I followed, my pulse thudding in my throat.

Braden stepped inside. The cold air followed him in, carrying the faint scent of salt and diesel from the bay.

He looked like a stranger.

His shirt was wrinkled, his tie half undone. His hair—usually perfect—was windblown, tangled from the bay breeze. His eyes were glassy, his face drawn and hollow.

I was about to unleash a torrent of questions, but all I could manage was, "I'm so glad you're okay" as I embraced him.

After a few seconds, I let him go. He tried to speak, but his voice cracked. For a heartbeat, he just stood there, the weight of whatever had happened pressing down on him. Then he crumpled.

Literally crumpled; his legs gave out under the weight of it all and his knees buckled. I caught him, or tried to, but we both sank to the floor.

"I'm sorry," he said. "God, Jenna, I'm so sorry."

Tears streaked down his face. I'd never seen him cry like that. Not when his father died. Not ever.

"What happened?" I whispered, my arms around him.

But he couldn't answer. He just kept shaking his head, as if begging me not to make him relive the worst day of his life.

For now, all I could do was hold him.

Later, I'd need answers. But in that moment, I only felt the fragile thud of his heart against mine. It was oddly reassuring. Proof that he was still here.

SEVEN

Madison dropped off Lucy at 9 p.m. She didn't press for details, knowing things around here were volatile, and that was putting it nicely.

Braden and I tried to put up a united, happy front for her, but she could tell something was off. Thankfully, her bedtime was at 9:30, and although she gave me a whiney "I just got home," I sent her to bed.

My husband showered and changed into an old Golden State Warriors 2015 championship hoodie and sweats. His hair was damp, his eyes bloodshot. He sat at the edge of the sofa, elbows on his knees, staring at the unlit fireplace like it owed him answers.

I brought him a cup of tea. The steam rose between us, thin and fragile.

"Talk to me," I said quietly. "Please."

He rubbed his palms together, the sound dry and nervous. "It's bad," he said finally. "Really bad."

I waited, giving him the time he needed.

"The merger's dead. Hudson pulled out. They said I missed deadlines, lost files. Documents that are just gone. Not on the servers, not in backup. Like they vanished. I missed the terms of the SLA." He looked up at me, eyes wide and pleading. "I didn't screw up, Jenna. I swear to God I didn't."

"Okay." I nodded slowly. "But that can't be why they fired you."

"The client fired the firm because of a screw-up under my watch," he said.

I understood that, but surely he'd earned enough good-will, having brought hundreds of millions of dollars in fees for the firm over eighteen years, that they wouldn't fire him over this. Would it damage his reputation, his career? Of course. But fired on the spot? It didn't make sense. It was not like he'd stolen; he'd screwed up.

He hesitated, as if he could tell what I was thinking. That pause was enough to make my stomach drop. There was more.

When he spoke again, he couldn't look at me. "There was something else."

The air thickened between us.

"My paralegal, Heather, filed a complaint," he said.

49

I knew she was involved in all this. He continued.

"She said I made her uncomfortable. Said I crossed a line."

My pulse started hammering. "What line?"

His head snapped up. "I didn't touch her." He said it too fast, too loud. "You have to believe me."

I didn't respond. I couldn't yet.

"She was the one who kept flirting with me," he continued, words spilling now, frantic. "Everyone saw it. She'd lean over my desk, laugh too hard at my dumb jokes. I ignored it and tried to keep things professional. When I finally told her to cut it out, suddenly files go missing, critical deadlines aren't met. Then I'm the one being inappropriate?"

He ran a hand through his hair, tugging at the ends. "Now they're calling it misconduct. Retaliation. Christ, Jenna, I've worked there eighteen years without a single complaint from anyone, male or female."

Like a man waiting for a verdict, he looked up at me. And I felt like a jury: unqualified, unwilling to be there, and divided.

My chest tightened. The room suddenly felt too small, the air too still. I wanted to reach for him, to make it all better. But the memory of that text—*We need to talk*—burned behind my eyelids.

"I didn't do anything," he said again, more quietly now. "You believe me, right?"

I reached out, covering his hand with mine. His skin was cold.

"I want to," I whispered. "But... there was a message from her. On your phone. It didn't sound like work."

His expression twisted, shock first, then guilt, then something darker. "You looked through my phone?"

"I saw it by accident. It was late. She texted you at ten o'clock at night when you were on the deck drinking."

He shook his head, the motion jerky. "She's lying. She's setting me up. Probably covering her own mistakes."

"But why you?" I asked.

"Because I'm the easy target. The partner with the corner office, in charge of the merger, and a family man with a reputation worth destroying. Maybe she thought I'd protect her if she screwed up. And when I didn't—when I held her accountable—she decided to take me down instead."

He looked so certain, so wounded. I wanted to believe him. God, I *needed* to believe him.

But somewhere deep inside, a whisper threaded through my thoughts: *Then why does it sound rehearsed? Like an attorney's closing statement...*

I squeezed his hand. "What happens now?"

"They're investigating to wrap up everything nice and tight, but the termination is final. And Peck made it clear— they're done with me. I'm radioactive." He laughed—a short, bitter sound. "Years of loyalty, and I'm out the door before lunch."

The laugh broke into something closer to a sob. He pressed the heels of his palms against his eyes. "I didn't even get to clear out my desk. My photographs of you and Lucy. They'll mail my life back to me in a box."

I slid closer, wrapping my arms around him. He felt rigid, hollowed out. For a moment, he didn't move, then he let out a shuddering breath and sank into me.

"We'll figure it out," I murmured. "We'll find you another firm."

Braden gave a small, defeated shake of his head. "It's not that simple. The rumor's already out there. By tomorrow, every partner in the city will know. No one wants a headline risk."

He sounded like a man reciting his own obituary.

I pressed my cheek to his shoulder. The smell of his shampoo seemed intimate. I remembered mornings when he smelled like this before work, when he'd kiss me goodbye and promise to be home by seven. That man felt light years away.

After a moment, I asked, "Why didn't you at least text me? I called and called. I thought something terrible happened."

He blinked, like he'd just remembered. "My phone's gone."

"What do you mean, gone?"

"I thought I left it in the car at the ferry lot, but it wasn't there when I checked. I must've dropped it somewhere between the ferry and the office. Or someone grabbed it. I don't know." He rubbed his forehead. "Honestly, I didn't have the strength to care."

I frowned. "You didn't have your work phone?"

"They took that too. Along with my laptop, keycard. Everything. I walked out of there with nothing but my wallet and an empty bag."

Something about the way he said it—flat, vacant—made the hairs on my arms stand up. A missing phone. The timing. The complaint. It all swirled together into something I couldn't quite name, but it didn't feel random.

"Maybe someone will turn it in," I said gently, though the words felt thin.

He didn't answer.

"Jenna," he said after a long pause, "you do believe me, don't you? About Heather?"

I hesitated, just long enough for him to notice.

His whole body stiffened. "Jesus," he whispered. "You think I did it."

"I didn't say that."

"You didn't have to." He pulled back, eyes flashing with hurt. "I'm telling you the truth."

"I'm trying," I said. "But you've been lying for weeks—shutting me out, drinking, you reject me in bed, barely talking. And now this comes out of nowhere. What am I supposed to think?"

Sighing hard, he ran his hands over his face. "I was trying to protect you. I didn't want to drag you into the mess."

"That's not protection, Braden. That's deception."

The words landed heavily between us. For a long time, neither of us spoke.

Finally, he said, "I'm sorry."

I nodded, though I wasn't sure what I was forgiving.

Outside, the wind picked up, rattling the windows. Seemed appropriate enough.

Braden leaned forward, elbows on his knees again. He looked like he might collapse all over again. "I'll call Greg tomorrow," he said. "Maybe there's still a chance to fight this."

"Okay," I said softly.

But my mind had already splintered in two: the wife who wanted to stand by him, and the woman who'd seen another woman's name light up on his phone late at night.

He reached for me again, resting his head against my shoulder. His breath hitched once, twice. "I didn't touch her," he whispered.

I closed my eyes. "I know."

But I wasn't sure I did.

When he finally fell asleep on the couch, his head heavy in my lap, I stared out through the window at the dark curve of the bay. A single huge cargo ship moved across the water, its lights faint and distant, heading towards the Pacific. Asia probably. The fantasy of being a stowaway on it danced around my head for a moment before I came back to reality.

I told myself we'd survive this. That the truth would come out.

But I wasn't sure I wanted the truth.

EIGHT

BRADEN FELL ASLEEP HARD, THE KIND OF SLEEP THAT is the sedated courtesy of Lorazepam and bourbon rather than a privilege of the living. I didn't know he had self-medicated until he began slurring his words. No point in arguing with him about that then, so I helped him to bed instead.

After everything he'd endured, he needed rest, and we both knew it wouldn't come naturally. I would have been fine with the prescription not mixing with the booze, but it worked. He was out in less than ten minutes, his breathing even, his body slack beneath the covers.

I watched his chest rise and fall; he seemed so peaceful now despite the tumultuous day he'd had, with a promise of more shitty days ahead. Slipping quietly out of the bedroom, I closed the door until only a sliver of hallway light cut through the dark. The house held its late-night quiet. The refrigerator's low electrical purr rose, then faded. Far off, a foghorn dragged its warning across the bay. I peeked into Lucy's room. Sunny lifted his head from the bed, blinked at me, yawned, and flopped back down. Lucy was asleep, her small hand resting on her stuffed dolphin.

Downstairs, I kept the lights off, using my phone flashlight until the faint under-cabinet glow in the kitchen guided me to the breakfast nook. I set down my laptop, a spiral notebook, and my favorite gel pen that always wrote smoothly.

I used to do this for a living, before Lucy, before school pickups and PTA sign-ups, before a marriage that now felt like something you maintained the way you maintained a yard.

At *GrayMatter Insights*, I was the one they called when the data didn't make sense — when a market looked steady but wasn't, when a competitor appeared out of nowhere. I knew how to triangulate truth away from noise. The muscles remembered, even if the title was gone.

I opened the laptop, and instinct took over. New browser profile. No extensions. Cache cleared. Search set to *verbatim*.

A few OSINT tools I hadn't touched in years blinked to life like old friends — state databases, professional networks, a people-finder I'd never admit using. I remembered the last time I did a deep dive like this, but it was too painful a memory, so I soldiered on with the task at hand. Who the hell is Heather Evans and why is she seemingly taking a wrecking ball to Braden's thus far charmed life?

I told myself this wasn't just snooping—because it was, but justified. I was being pragmatic.

HEATHER EVANS, I typed. The commonness of that name was a challenge. I added the firm name and city.

Too broad.

A thousand results bloomed like weeds. I refined it: "Heather Evans" + San Francisco + paralegal.

Better.

Her LinkedIn appeared third. Private enough to look modest, public enough to serve its purpose on the site.

Banner photo: the San Francisco skyline at dusk.

Headline: *Paralegal | Corporate Transactions | M&A Support.*

Neat. Restrained. Yet it displayed confidence.

I clicked *About*.

BA, University of Oregon — Sociology, minor in Econ.

Paralegal Certificate, San Francisco City College.

Volunteer: CASA (court-appointed special advocate). Two years listed, no photos.

Endorsements: Document management. E-discovery. Client interface.

She was young, just twenty-three, so she could not put much on her account. What there was seemed so vanilla and clean. Curated as to not really stand out. As if scrubbed and rebuilt by someone who wanted to be both visible and invisible.

But maybe I was just imagining things.

I double clicked on her headshot and opened it in a new tab so I could see the original larger-sized photograph.

It was clearly professional — shot from a high angle, soft light smoothing every line. Brown hair, parted center, soft waves brushing her shoulders. Clean makeup: mascara, nude lip, faint shimmer on the cheekbones.

She was beautiful. Polished. Familiar.

I stared, a small chill prickling under my skin.

Although she didn't look like me — not exactly —I could see what a lazy eye might decide. Same bone structure. Same hair color. Younger. Brighter. The version of me Braden once married.

If the allegations were true, maybe that was his type. And he was trading me in for a younger model.

I wasn't sure if that should flatter or devastate me.

It's not about me. I shook those thoughts of insecurity and self-loathing away. I downloaded the headshot and dropped it into PimEyes, a paid reverse-image search that was like Google Images on steroids.

Her digital footprint was practically non-existent for a twenty-three-year-old. That was odd. Aside from the LinkedIn profile and an Instagram private account, which meant that only approved followers could access its posts and images, there wasn't much to go on.

No personal website, no other social handles, no forgotten Tumblr account. No tagged photos at some frat house in college. It seemed scrubbed. Both accounts I did find had been opened less than a year before she applied for the job at Braden's law firm. It was as if she'd set up LinkedIn and Instagram accounts knowing that not having those might be a red flag.

It all seemed so controlled. Deliberate.

Smart. Or maybe she was just into her privacy. I had read about the younger generations eschewing the social media world they were born into, unlike previous generations like mine that chose to surrender our privacy to the tech companies.

I clicked her *Activity* tab on LinkedIn. A few reposts from paralegal associations, a diligence checklist article, two congratulatory comments. Then, six months ago:

"Excited to join the corporate legal team at Langford, Hayes & Fox. Looking forward to learning from the best."

A handful of likes. No office photos. No coworkers tagged.

Nothing accidental.

I moved deeper. The university registry, alumni notes with an announcement that she had relocated to San Francisco for paralegal studies.

So Oregon checked out.

City College's legal certificate page took forever to

load, the PDF margins crooked and compressed. I zoomed in until I found her name: *Evans, Heather R.*

I looked up her paralegal license; it was active. She seemed legit, so nothing shady there. Verification. Proof that wasn't proof at all — just another breadcrumb in a maze she'd built for snoopers like me to find.

Leaning back, I rubbed my eyes until sparks flared behind them. Most young people left a long trail of selfies, memes, and bad tweets. Heather Evans had left nothing.

The floor creaked behind me and I jumped, then let out a relieved breath when I realized it was just the house settling.

I was about to shut down and head to bed, when my phone trilled against the table, starling me. Who could be calling this late?

UNKNOWN CALLER.

Normally, I would've ignored it. But after the last twenty-four hours, every unknown felt personal.

"Hello?"

Silence.

"Who is this?"

A breath. Close to the mic to let me know someone was there. Then a voice, robotic, distorted. The caller was obviously altering it.

"Good night," the weird voice said, creeping the hell out of me.

The line went dead.

I couldn't even tell if it belonged to a man or a woman. But something in the cadence—the pause before hanging up— made my gut tell me the creepy caller was female.

With goosebumps running up and down my arms, I looked around. It felt as if the caller had been watching me, knowing what I was doing.

Heather? I thought. This ordeal was already driving me crazy.

I stared at the screen until it dimmed back to my home photo: Lucy and Sunny at Stinson Beach brought me comfort. Then my mind went into analyst mode, cataloging the obvious.

Someone had my number.

Someone wanted me to hear them.

Could've been a wrong number. A prank. A drunk dial.

But that seemed way too convenient, and I provided myself with far-fetched possibilities to wave off the call as nothing directed at me.

"Good night," I whispered, testing the words, hating the way they sounded in my mouth.

I took my pen and wrote: **TIMELINE.**

Then I drew a line across the page and began marking events in quick strokes before my courage faded.

— Six months ago: Heather joined the firm.

— Recently: Braden starts drinking, pulling away from me.

— Last week: Unknown calls (twice? three times?). Not sure if I ignored them or forgot.

— Last night: Heather texted Braden: *We need to talk.*

— Today: Merger fails. HR complaint. Braden fired.

— Tonight: Braden was missing for hours. Phone missing too.

— 12:41 a.m.: Unknown caller. Altered voice: "Good night."

What did it mean? Probably nothing. I was getting all worked up in my head as I kept going through my notes, over and over.

What do I have to show? A big nothing burger, as Braden would say.

Still, I felt my pulse quicken. *You know that's not true.*

I'd had enough. I shut the laptop. The clock read 1:03.

Upstairs, the house was still, aside from the gentle breath of a sleeping Lucy. I paused at the bedroom doorway; Braden was snoring loudly thanks to the pill and the bourbon. I let my eyes adjust for a moment and made my way to bed. Braden rolled over to his side. Mercifully, that ended the snoring.

His empty TUMI bag sat on the floor beside the bed, folded in like a collapsed trap.

I wanted to believe him so badly. I closed my eyes for a second before he began to snore again, so loudly that I lay there wide awake, wondering.

What had really gone down between him and Heather?

NINE

MORNING CAME BRIGHT AND WRONG.

The light pouring through the curtains was too clean, too ordinary for what our lives had become overnight. I moved through the kitchen on autopilot, every motion rehearsed—grinding coffee, slicing fruit, spreading avocado on toast. My body remembered the choreography even if my mind was still trapped in last night's wreckage.

Braden sat at the counter, wearing a fresh shirt. His eyes were ringed with dark circles, his shoulders caved in. He looked so tired, though he'd got eight hours of deep sleep. It was one of the reasons he didn't like taking those pills; they left him fighting off a brain fog for most of the morning.

He tried for a smile when Lucy bounded down the stairs, hair still damp from her shower, backpack swinging off one shoulder.

"Morning, chickadee," he said softly.

"Morning, Daddy." She grinned, oblivious to the quiet tension clogging the air.

We'd both promised, wordlessly, that Lucy wouldn't see the cracks. No matter what. So we smiled. We joked about her cereal getting soggy and about how Sunny was still snoring under the table. We looked like a family again. Almost.

"Can we go early?" Lucy asked. "I want to show Chase the sea glass I found."

"Sure," I said, forcing myself to sound bright. "Finish your cereal and juice."

Braden glanced at me over the rim of his mug, gratitude and exhaustion blending in his eyes. Last night we'd fallen asleep tangled in silence, not touching but not turning away either.

I dropped Lucy off at school every day, but today Braden insisted on coming since he wouldn't be getting on the ferry for work this morning or in the foreseeable future. It was a ritual he rarely was able to participate in.

We took my Porsche Cayenne, and I drove. Braden was still dealing with the mental fogginess from the pills and a head-crushing hangover from the bourbon.

The ride was quiet. Lucy hummed along with the radio, swinging her legs. Braden looked out the window, jaw tight, eyes flicking back to me and Lucy every few seconds. He managed a sad smile.

I wondered what came next; meetings with attorneys, calls from HR, whatever fallout still waited. I'm sure that was heavy on his mind as well.

"You okay?" I asked quietly.

He nodded once. "Yeah. Just tired."

A lie, but one I let slide.

We pulled into the circular drive in front of Vista Bay Elementary. Kids in puffy jackets darted across the sidewalk, parents waved, teachers wrangled backpacks and lunchboxes.

Braden got out first, helping Lucy with her bag.

The normalcy of it all was surreal. But anything out of the ordinary stood out like a sore thumb, and Braden's presence there did just that. The usual close-knit pack of Marin County women decked out in *rich mom* aesthetic stood there watching. I doubt they knew what was going on—yet; it was the novelty of seeing Braden at the drop off. And by the way they were ogling him, his handsome face and fit body probably played a big part in them staring.

"Big day?" he asked Lucy.

She nodded. "We're making volcanoes in science."

"Explosive," he said, and she giggled at the dad joke.

He crouched to kiss her cheek, holding her for a moment longer than usual. "Love you, chickadee."

"Love you too, Daddy."

Madison caught my eye across the drive, confusion on

67

her face. I gave a small shake of my head. *Later.* She understood and nodded back.

Lucy turned and ran toward the steps, joining Chase and other friends, proudly showing them the sea glass she had found the other day when we were walking by the beach shoreline area along Blackies Pasture. That seemed a lifetime ago.

Braden and I stood watching until she disappeared inside. The smile on his face collapsed as soon as she was gone.

I reached for his hand, meaning to say something—anything—that would keep him from unraveling again. But I never got the chance.

A man was walking toward us from the parking lane. Early forties, friendly face, Patagonia fleece, clipboard tucked under one arm.

He looked like every other dad here; frat boy, clean-cut, harmless. I figured he was one of the volunteer parents that helped keep the morning drop-off flowing smoothly. They didn't like it when parents leave the cars unattended for too long.

"Braden Morrissey?" he asked pleasantly.

Braden turned, wary. "Yeah?"

"This is for you." The man handed him a thick manila envelope.

"What's this?"

The man's expression was polite, professional. "You've been served."

Braden just stared. The words seemed to take a few seconds to land.

"Have a good day," the man said, already walking off, checking his phone.

"What the hell—" Braden started, but he broke off. He tore the flap open, scanning the first page. Color drained from his face.

"What is it?" I asked.

He handed it to me with shaking fingers. The header read:

SUPERIOR COURT OF CALIFORNIA, COUNTY OF SAN FRANCISCO
Summons and Complaint
Attached: **Temporary Restraining Order**

I blinked, trying to make sense of the words swimming in front of me. "She filed a TRO?"

He nodded slowly, like he could barely believe it himself. "Heather. Jesus Christ."

A sound escaped me, half gasp, half scoff. Around us, the schoolyard noise seemed suddenly amplified: children laughing, the bell ringing, the squeak of sneakers on pavement. The ordinary world carried on while ours tilted sideways.

Two moms of Lucy's classmates who had been ogling

Braden, stood beside their Teslas, Peet's cups in hand. They'd watched everything. The leader of the clique, Cara, gave me a pitying smirk, her tone syrupy and sharp. "Ouch."

Her lapdog giggled behind her cup.

Braden stood frozen, still clutching the papers like they might dissolve if he held them long enough.

"Let's go," I said quietly, steering him toward the car.

The walk felt endless. Every step was heavy with the weight of what had just happened. Every parent we passed seemed to be watching while pretending not to.

Inside the car, I shut the door, shutting out the world's noise. "Braden, what does this mean?"

He stared at the dashboard. "It means she's doubling down. Not only did she file a sexual harassment complaint with the firm that got me fired, she's now filed a lawsuit against me."

I swallowed hard. "But you said—"

"I didn't do anything," he snapped, then immediately closed his eyes. "I'm sorry. I just... I can't believe this is happening."

The papers trembled in his lap. A coffee stain marred the top corner, and for some reason that detail undid me. It made it all too real.

Outside, the sun glinted off the playground. Lucy was somewhere inside, learning about volcanoes and laughing with her friends, unaware that her father's world was collapsing just a few feet away and that he was taking us down with him.

Braden looked out the windshield, jaw tight. "I should've seen this coming," he said quietly. "Some fine lawyer I am, that I let them serve me at Lucy's school. Bastards."

His tone was going from defeated to angry.

I started the car and drove off. Braden began thumbing through the complaint.

"Now what?" I asked.

"I need an attorney who handles this kind of thing."

"Do you know anyone?"

He didn't hesitate. "Emily Acosta."

"The degenerate movie producer's lawyer?" I asked, stunned.

Emily Acosta had made national news when she was hired to be the defense attorney for a disgraced A-list movie producer and got him off. That case had cemented her reputation for defending the indefensible. And that was who Braden wanted?

He nodded grimly. "She's ruthless. I need ruthless."

I didn't argue. There was nothing left to say.

The silence that followed us back home was suffocating.

When we reached the house, I went straight to the kitchen, set the envelope on the counter, and stared at it. The legal header, the stamped case number, the neat typeface. It was all so sterile for something that could destroy a life.

Braden poured himself a drink, though it was barely past nine.

"Don't," I said quietly.

He looked at me, eyes raw. "I need something to stop the shaking."

I didn't argue.

Outside, the day had turned bright and perfect. The kind of California morning that made the bay sparkle. Inside, everything felt gray.

I went upstairs, needing distance. From him. From all of it.

At the bedroom window, the bridge shimmered through the morning haze.

How well did I even know my husband? Lies, secrets, silences.

My reflection stared back from the glass.

Who was I to judge?

My secret could end this marriage all by itself.

TEN

Braden was already on his second drink when I went downstairs.

He was out on the deck, elbows resting on the railing, staring down at the bay like it might hand him answers if he waited long enough.

On the dining room table, the entire summons and complaint had been fanned out in neat rows—thirty, maybe forty pages—each a wrecking ball tearing down what was left of our formal life.

I moved closer, my eyes catching the bold header across the first page:

Heather Evans v. Langford, Hayes & Fox LLP, and Braden A. Morrissey.

The charges blurred as I read—*Harassment. Retaliation. Intentional Infliction of Emotional Distress.*

And below that, stapled to the end, the restraining

order: *Temporary. No contact. Mandatory surrender of firearms.*

My hand trembled as I reached for the page. If the accusations were true, Braden was not the man I thought I knew. The man I'd fallen in love with and married. The father of my child.

This all tugged loose a memory from my teenage years I didn't want to revisit. It belonged to someone else, some reckless young girl I'd shed long ago.

I exhaled slowly, steadying myself. No use digging up ghosts.

My attention drifted to the exhibits—photocopies of what looked like text messages, screenshots, and near the back, a glossy packet labeled *EVIDENCE: VISUAL EXHIBITS*.

I flipped it open.

Photographs.

High-definition.

Crisp, professional angles.

And there he was: Braden, sitting outside a Market Street restaurant. *Niza Café*. We'd been there countless times for brunch and dinners over the years.

He wasn't alone. Braden's head tilted toward a young brunette across the table. *Heather Evans.*

The way she leaned in, just enough for the table to be the only thing separating them. It wasn't overtly romantic, but it was intimate.

His smile was easy, unguarded. The kind of smile I hadn't seen in months.

The fact that he'd taken her there, to *our place,* made something twist deep in my chest. A nausea crept up my throat. I felt sick. But there were more photographs.

A different angle, closer. Braden's mouth shaped mid-word. Heather's lips parted, attentive. They could've been discussing trial exhibits. Or planning an affair. For all I knew, they had been screwing just before and felt ravenous. So he'd taken her there for an after-sex meal. A place he had taken me.

The third photo landed the final blow: Heather leaning in, her fingers resting lightly on his jacket lapel, Braden not stepping back. The lens had caught the moment like a prize.

I put the photographs down. My heartbeat crawled into my ears.

The world narrowed to those images. The sunlight on their faces, the faint intimacy of their gathering. Braden's hand wasn't touching her, but it didn't have to. The picture told its own story.

Behind me, the sliding door creaked.

"Jenna," Braden said, sounding fragile.

I turned, holding up the photos. "When was this taken?"

He blinked, confused, then wary. "I don't know. It's not what it looks like."

My pulse thudded. "It looks like you're having lunch with the woman accusing you of harassment. Don't tell me it was for work. I'm not stupid."

"I went there alone for a quick bite," he said tiredly. "She showed up. Asked if she could join me. Said she had questions about the merger. I said fine, but it became obvious it was bullshit. She started hitting on me. Propositioned me outright. I told her no. She got upset."

"Upset? You were smiling."

"That was taken right after she sat down. I was being polite. Friendly. Until she started coming on to me. That was right before I told her off. It's convenient for her that there aren't any photos of that. Of me shutting her down, telling her I'd reassign her once the merger was done. Her storming off, upset. Why aren't those photos included?"

I couldn't stop looking at the photos.

"Because it doesn't fit her bullshit story," he said, answering his own question.

He sounded so sincere. But that didn't mean anything. Cheating spouses lie. It's what they do.

"She's lying," he said again, almost pleading. "She's twisting everything. That meeting. It wasn't personal. She showed up. I think she was stalking me, setting me up. Who even took those photos? And why?"

I wanted to believe him. God, I wanted to. I looked at the angle of the shots. They were taken from across Market Street, maybe from the curbside platform for the Muni Fline. A clean line of sight. It seemed convenient that a photographer should be there. Why?

But the *why* didn't matter. The photograph didn't lie.

For weeks I'd worried for him, felt sorry for him. But as I looked at that photo, the pity began to evaporate.

A heat rose in me—slow, molten, dangerous. The kind that had no outlet, only pressure. My sadness cracked under it, giving way to something older, sharper. Rage.

"I have stood by you," I said, my voice trembling. "Through the drinking, through the silence, through every unanswered question. And now. *This*? It's too much, Braden."

He set the glass down too hard. The sound splintered the air between us. "I didn't sleep with her!"

"But you met her. You let her close enough that she could do this." I gestured to the pile of documents that now defined our lives.

His eyes glistened, desperate. "I made a mistake trusting her, but that's it."

When I said nothing, he turned away, walking back out to the deck, gripping the railing so tightly his knuckles went white.

Angry as I was, it worried me. I joined him outside. I wanted to tell him I believed him, but the words wouldn't come. Because I didn't.

I stood behind him in silence.

"She's ruined my life," he said, not turning around. "Everything I've worked for. Gone."

"Not just you," I said quietly.

He froze. I heard him sigh, the glass clinking faintly as he lifted it and took a long drink.

I walked back inside, leaving him with his bourbon. My hands were trembling, but my steps stayed steady.

On the table, Heather's photograph stared up at me as if she were taunting me.

What was her end game? Could it just be greed? Suing a Morrissey trust-fund baby?

There seemed to be more to all this than money. She could have had her attorney try for a quick settlement. A legal shakedown, so to speak. Why go right into filing a lawsuit?

It seemed she was hell-bent on destroying him. Lucy and I were collateral. I felt a rage I hadn't known in a long time.

ELEVEN

THEY CALLED IT *INTAKE,* LIKE I WAS BEING PROCESSED
through a machine. And I suppose in a sense I was. I was
being shuttled from one state-run machine, the foster care
system, to another: the juvenile justice center.

Girls wearing orange scrubs, wrists cuffed, sneakers
squeaking on the waxed linoleum, stood in line. The air
smelled like bleach and tears.

They put us in a holding cell for the evaluation stage of
the process. Poorly paid and overworked state shrinks tried
to figure out what to do with us during our incarceration.

Most people knew the adult prison system had just
about forgotten the part about rehabilitation. But when it
came to the juvenile prison, they still wanted to believe
that kids could be saved.

A woman with a clipboard came up to the bars where

ten of us sat on the concrete bench lining the wall. Nothing to do but sit, size each other up, and think.

I'd had a lot of time to think since I'd pulled that trigger. A lot of time to learn.

The stocky woman with the clipboard and bad skin called my name. I stood, the cell door clanged open. A CO took my arm while two others escorted me down a long corridor washed by bright lights pouring down from the ceiling panels.

They took me down to an interview room. It was a little bigger than the one where the cops had questioned me when I was first arrested. Inside, there was a metallic desk with a deep dent on the front panel. I wondered if some other youth had sat where I sat and taken out his anger on that desk.

A polite cough got my attention. I looked up at a man in his late twenties sitting behind the desk. He was good-looking, surrounded by stacks of folders. He ignored me for a moment, tapping away on his laptop.

Finally, he looked up and smiled. "I'm the intake screener," he said, launching into a speech about placement and safety and compliance. Blah, blah, blah.

I watched his mouth move but tuned out the words. I was already studying him, figuring out my angle. It was a skill I was still learning.

He was polite, but I could tell he just wanted to get

through that stack, pass me along, and move on to the next girl waiting in holding.

I went with the scared-first-timer act—the wounded gazelle surrounded by lions.

But in reality, I was the fucking lion.

My fingers drifted to the thin scar on my wrist, the one I kept hidden. A reminder of how far I'd let him break me once. Never again.

While in holding, I had been closing my eyes tightly over and over, so now they looked glassy, a little red. Perfect. I knew I was above-average in the looks department. Beautiful, hot, all that bullshit. Boys always sought me out. Girls too. And men, like that pig I'd killed. I was learning how to use that to my advantage so I didn't end up under the thumb of someone like my foster father ever again.

We went through the motions.

"Any mental health issues? Drug use? Suicidal thoughts?"

I gave him what he wanted—quiet, broken *yeses* and *nos* in all the right places. He liked that. They liked damaged. It made them feel like saviors.

The truth was, I wasn't broken. Not in the way they thought. It was their system that was broken. And I had finally figured out how to use it to my advantage.

They took my shoelaces, my hair tie, my freedom. I didn't fight it. I was already learning that fights were expensive, and I didn't yet know the currency here. But I would.

They placed me in the general population, which was exactly what I wanted.

I was expecting the prison to look like the one in *The Shawshank Redemption*, but it looked like a college dorm. And that was even what they called our cells: dorm rooms. But there was no sugarcoating where we were. And all of us here were broken in one way or the other. I suppose the same could be said about a college campus. Just that those kids had their freedom and didn't know how good they got it.

The noise was constant—TV blaring, laughter too loud, arguments that turned sharp and fast. The girls were wolves with manicures, and I watched them from my bunk, clocking who was soft and who stared too long. The tough ones bragged about what they'd done. The soft ones cried into their pillows. The guards pretended not to hear.

I didn't cry. Not because I was tough; I just couldn't. It was always tough for me to show emotions or get emotional. I usually just mimicked others to seem normal.

But I practiced because crying was useful in the system, and on the outside.

At night, I'd sneak into the bathroom after lights out. There was a mirror cracked across the middle, distorting my reflection into two halves. I'd stand there and practice.

A quiver in the lip. A tremble in the chin. The single

tear that made even the hardest people soften. Seven seconds flat—tears on cue.

By the end of the month, I had it down to five. I was getting good at it.

When the staff came by with their clipboards, I gave them the version of me they wanted: scared but hopeful. I told them I'd made a mistake, that I wanted to be better. I talked about second chances. About redemption. About faith. How sorry I was about killing that poor man—I had to swallow back my bile on that; how I should have gone to the police, instead of doing what I did. I had no right. Blah, blah, blah.

The dummies ate it up. They nodded, patted my shoulder, told me I was brave.

I told them fear.

I told myself triumph.

The other girls saw through it quickly. They knew the act and admired how well I was playing the game. One of the girls laughed so hard she almost fell off her bunk. Monalisa Guerra was around the same age and height as me, but from the way she carried herself and the respect she got from the other inmates, it didn't take me long to figure out she was one of the alphas. A leader. She took a liking to me, which I found reassuring. It was good to have a friend like Monalisa Guerra here.

"Damn, Meryl Streep," she said. "You got them wrapped around your finger already."

The name stuck.

"Meryl" got extra dessert.

"Meryl" got a cushy office job.

"Meryl" could cry in front of the social worker and get commissary points while the rest of them got scolded.

Every day I learned something new about power: how to make people believe you were harmless, how to turn guilt into currency, how to smile while you lied.

They thought I was rehabilitating.

I was learning how to be a wolf in a henhouse.

TWELVE

THE MORNING AFTER BEING SERVED AND SEEING THOSE photographs felt like I had woken up with a hangover that could rival Braden's, but sans the pills and bourbon.

It had been a fitful night. Mean-mom Cara's catty *"ouch"* echoed in my head. The delighted look on her face, and that of her minion, continued mocking me. I hated giving her the space in there. Our private disaster was probably being picked apart at every Vista Bay coffee shop by now.

I kept replaying the photographs over and over until they came to life in my head, like an old grainy 8mm movie. Braden and Heather at the restaurant. Laughing, smiling, flirting. Then images of their faces in the throws of ecstasy until mercifully I woke up in a cold sweat.

By the time the sun broke over the crest, my head

throbbed and my nerves stretched taut, fine as piano wire. I got out of bed, eager for that terrible movie in my head to stop.

Braden left at nine to meet with Emily Acosta. She had an office in San Francisco.

I'd looked her up. She had an impressive background. Yale Law, former federal prosecutor, now one of the city's most sought-after defenders for men accused of harassment and worse.

"Doesn't hiring her make you look guilty?" I had asked him last night.

"She gets results. There is no sugarcoating that," he had replied.

Men accused of sex crimes, I'd read, liked to hire women to soften them for juries by sending them a subliminal message: certainly a man who abuses women wouldn't hire one to represent him.

I didn't know if that was true, but I couldn't shake it. Had Braden thought that too? Did he think like one of them because... he was one of *them*? I shivered at the thought.

Why had Emily Acosta, once a federal prosecutor, built her private practice around defending predators like that disgusting movie producer? Seemed like a strange calling for a woman, planting her flag on the wrong side of #MeToo.

I supposed her $1200-an-hour rate helped ease that kind of moral dilemmas.

Good thing that a now unemployed Braden still had access to the Morrissey trust fund.

He wanted me to come with him. To show unity. I refused. I told him it would look better if he handled it alone, but the truth was simpler. I couldn't sit next to him pretending we were still a team when I was having my doubts. I wanted to believe, to support him, but it was too much, too fast. I just needed time to think, alone.

I GOT BACK HOME after dropping Lucy off at school. She was blissfully unaware, thank God, but I figured that would be short lived. The only group crueler than a gaggle of bored rich housewives like Cara was kids. As soon as they got wind of what was happening with Braden and me, they were going to let her have it. I thought of pulling her out of school until this blew over, but I decided against it, for the moment.

The house was too quiet. Even Sunny seemed uneasy, following me from room to room like he sensed something had changed. I always said he was a little empath wanting to take our emotional pain.

Braden took the lawsuit papers with him, but I'd made copies while he slept.

I laid them out on the dining table like he had done with the originals. The photographs were tucked inside a folder now, but that didn't help. I could not unsee them. Braden's easy smile, her bright eyes, the way she leaned in close, like they were a lunch date, not a business one.

Now I needed to be rational, analytical, methodical, like I used to be when I worked at GrayMatter Insights. Back then, I could turn chaos into an easy-to-follow pattern.

So I opened my notebook—the same one I'd started the night of that eerie phone call—and began building a timeline.

TIMELINE — Working Draft

Six months ago: Heather joined the firm

Three months ago: Braden started drinking heavily. Withdraws from me

Two months ago: Missed deadlines began.

One month ago: Braden's behavior worsens—snaps, disappears for hours

Last week: "We need to talk" text from Heather

This week: Braden fired. TRO filed

Today: Meeting with Emily Acosta

I looked at my notes. Neat. Linear. Too neat.

It looked like the kind of story you tell when you want to sound believable.

Was it Heather's fabrication or Braden's?

Things became easier when I thought I knew the truth. But now everything felt like a setup.

By whom, though? And why?

Heather could've built this case with surgical precision with fake texts, manipulated images, fabricated timelines. She could've planned every beat.

But maybe she didn't have to.

Maybe she'd just told the truth. And it was Braden using a sleight of hand to obfuscate the simple fact that he'd had an affair with his subordinate and began to harass her when she ended it, as she alleged in her suit.

That was a possibility that made my throat tighten.

Because if Heather was truthful, then Braden had lied. Again.

And if he lied about her, what else had he lied about?

I pressed my fingers to my temples. The idea of Braden —my husband, Lucy's father—not only cheating but threatening and harassing a woman for ending their affair made me sick. His secrets and lies made me sick.

I felt like such a hypocrite. But I had to remind myself this wasn't about me; it was about him. He'd brought this to our home, to our family, not me. Men had always been the same. They promised, they smiled, they made you feel safe —until the moment they didn't. Every man before Braden had proven it in their own way. Now he, too?

Different faces, same story.

I'd convinced myself Braden was the exception. I was such a fool. Why would he be any different?

It was half past noon. I should've gone for a run, done something. Instead, I sat there, staring at the lawsuit, at the photographs, at my timeline as if the answers were hiding between the lines.

I didn't have any music on. I liked the silence when I was thinking.

So when my phone went off, the sound jolted through me like a gunshot.

UNKNOWN NUMBER

For a second, I thought it might be the same creepy caller from last night. But it wasn't a phone call; it was a text.

I hesitated, then opened it.

Ask him about Tahoe in April

That was it. No punctuation. No follow-up. Just that.

My stomach dropped.

Tahoe.

We had a lakefront cabin there. It was our perfect escape from the city. Winters spent skiing, summers on the water. A place that had always felt like our own Fortress of Solitude.

I checked my calendar. We hadn't gone up there in April. I wasn't sure what this text was implying, or who the hell was behind it.

I texted back:

Who is this?

I waited. One minute, two. Nothing.

No reply. Not even the dots that show someone's typing.

Just the message sitting there, unanswered, like a dare.

Ask him about Tahoe in April

My eyes drifted back to the documents spread across the table.

I pulled the photograph of Braden and Heather at Niza Café from the folder; a place he used to take me. Had he taken her to Tahoe, too? To our cabin?

My stomach churned. It hurt.

I grabbed my phone and flipped through back to my calendar with one hand, the photograph trembling in the other.

Sure enough, we hadn't been up there that month, but Braden had been on a "business trip" during the second week of April. A conference held at The Ritz-Carlton near Truckee. Just a short drive from the cabin.

I dropped the phone onto the table. My fingers were shaking.

The screen still glowed beside the photograph, that text shining back at me like a dangerous truth that I didn't want to know about, but I needed to know. I grabbed my laptop and logged into the cabin's smart-home dashboard. Maybe I was looking for proof, or maybe I was hoping to be wrong.

The interface loaded slowly. The familiar map of our Lake Tahoe property, the security camera thumbnails, the smart-lock history.

A guest code had been created in mid-April. Deleted two days later.

My pulse kicked.

I clicked into the video-feed archives. Most clips were innocuous, just shadows shifting in the entryway, a spider doing its thing by the camera lens, snow melt dripping from the roof. A squirrel zipping by. Then one thumbnail caught my eye. It was a twelve-second clip from the same week of the business trip.

I hit play.

There were two people, but I couldn't see their faces since the recording didn't pick them up until the cabin door opened and one of them was already inside.

"You're gonna love this place," a male voice said. I recognized it. My blood pressure dropped. I couldn't see his face, but I knew his voice. It was Braden.

The camera's angle was tight, showing only part of his shoulder, then a woman walked into the frame. Brown hair. Slim build. She was looking around like one does when visiting a new home. As she turned to look around the entryway, she glanced up at the camera. It was Heather Evans.

The video ended there.

I replayed it twice, then closed the laptop with shaking

hands. Whatever truth I'd been trying to build in my neat little timeline shattered right then.

That rage—the one I thought I'd buried years ago—came back full-force, hot and alive beneath my skin.

That two-timing son of a bitch.

I walked away from the table like it was on fire. I didn't want to look at those documents—or those photographs—anymore.

As I stepped out onto the deck, the Alcatraz ferry glided by headed toward the island that had once held the worst criminals in the country. It now crawled with selfie-taking tourists from all over the world, its very own kitschy gift shop full of faux prison-related items. Cups, food trays, utensils made to look like the items inmates had used back in the day. For $29.99 you too could drink from a cup like Al Capone's. Except this one was mass-produced in China.

Kite surfers and sailboats glided across the water, carefree and bright against the afternoon haze.

I imagined myself on one of those sail boats, wind in my hair, a glass of good wine in hand, an indulgent charcuterie board spread out beside me. The boat cut west, past the Golden Gate Strait, out toward the Pacific just like the cargo ship. Once again, I was on that boat. Leaving all this behind.

Sailing away somewhere warm. Somewhere no one knew my name. Or my past.

A clean slate. A new life.

I'd done it before.

Then I looked down into the backyard and saw Lucy's jump rope coiled in the grass, pink handles gleaming in the sun. The fantasy melted away.

There was no starting over. Not anymore.

THIRTEEN

BRADEN CAME HOME JUST AFTER SIX.

The front door opened and I heard the steady thump of his shoes, confident, measured—the sound of someone who'd gotten his swagger back.

When he stepped into the kitchen, he looked like a man reborn. Crisp shirt, clean shave, fresh bravado.

"She's taking the case," he said before I could speak. "Emily Acosta is a killer. And she believes me." I don't think he said that to slight me, but it stung. He continued. "She's putting together a response and motion to dissolve the TRO. She thinks it's all going to fall apart once we get in front of a judge. Heather is going to regret her false claims against me. The firm too. For wrongful termination."

I didn't say anything. I just watched him drop his

leather briefcase on the counter and loosen his tie like he'd won something.

"She told me not to panic," he went on. "The main thing is to preserve everything. Texts, emails, files. Don't delete anything. And we have to obey the TRO to the letter. No contact with Heather, direct or indirect."

He poured himself a drink, the casualness of the motion making my skin itch.

"There'll be a status hearing soon," he said, taking a sip. "But the key right now is optics. We don't escalate publicly. We don't talk about it to anyone. No comments, no statements, no social media. Total black out. That's her advice."

I let out a low breath. "So we sit quietly while she drags your name—and mine—through the mud?"

He looked at me like I'd missed the point. "It's temporary. The less noise we make, the better. She said that's how you win these things so we control the narrative, stay composed. Teddy Roosevelt style: 'Speak softly and carry a big stick'."

It sounded an awful lot like surrender. Like what the rich sex offenders do. Bully and pay their accusers into silence. But I didn't say anything. I hadn't been sure how I would feel at seeing him after that Tahoe video. I felt anger.

Braden mistook my silence for compliance. "She's good, Jenna. She'll handle it. You'll see."

I folded my arms.

"Where's Lucy?" he asked.

"She's spending the night at Madison's place."

He seemed surprised about that since we hadn't discussed it. We hadn't, because it was last minute. I didn't want Lucy here, not tonight.

His puzzled look morphed into a sly smile.

"So, we have the whole house to ourselves," he purred.

The nerve. *Now he wants me?*

"I don't think so." My arms are folded even more tightly across my chest.

"What's wrong?" he asked with a furrowed brow.

The words detonated inside me.

"What's wrong?" I repeated, laughing bitterly. "You really want to ask me that?"

He flinched. "Jenna—"

"What's wrong is that our daughter's school drop-off turned into a public humiliation. What's wrong is that your face is now attached to a lawsuit accusing you of sexual harassment and retaliation. What's wrong is that I've spent the last forty-eight hours not knowing if I'm married to an innocent man or a liar who's been screwing his paralegal at our favorite café and our cabin!"

He set his glass down too fast; the bourbon sloshed over the rim. "It's not like that."

"Then what *is* it like?" I snapped.

"Wait. The cabin? What are you talking about?"

I crossed to the table, flipped open my laptop, and spun it toward him.

"Watch."

Braden leaned closer, squinting at the screen as the security video from the Tahoe cabin entryway played. His voice said, *"You're gonna love this place."* The woman's shoulder is just inside the frame. Then she looks around and there she is, clear as day, Heather Evans, entering our cabin.

Color drained from his face. He reached for the laptop and watched it again. Then again.

Finally, he said, "That's not me."

I stared at him. "Excuse me?"

He gestured at the screen, his voice rising. "That's not me, Jenna. Look at the date, April fifteenth. I was at a client conference at the Ritz that week. I was so busy that I didn't even stop at the cabin. I drove straight back to the city."

Before I could open my mouth, he added, "You couldn't even see my face in that video. Could be anyone."

"That's your voice," I said coldly. "And there is no denying that it was Heather. In our cabin. Inside!"

He shook his head. "I can see it's her. But she wasn't there with me, because I wasn't there. She must have broken in with someone else."

I clicked on the smart-lock log. "They didn't have to break in. Explain this."

A new code entry, created mid-April. Deleted two days later.

"Only an admin can do that," I said. "And we're the only two admins. I sure as hell didn't set up that code."

"Neither did I!" he said, sounding defensive.

"Stop lying!" I shouted.

"I don't know what's going on. But I swear that wasn't me. She must have hacked—"

I interrupted him. "Stop. You make her sound like she's a Bond villain."

"Jenna, please." He stepped closer. "I swear to God, it wasn't me. You have to believe me."

Part of me softened. Should I believe him? I wanted to so badly. But enough was enough.

"I can't," I said quietly.

He froze. "What are you saying?"

"I need time, Braden. Away from all this," I said, waving my hands towards the laptop and court papers strewn on her dining room table. "Away from you."

The look he gave me of shock and sadness almost made me want to take it back. But I couldn't.

I took a deep breath. "I want you to move out. Tonight."

He stared at me like I'd slapped him. "You're kicking me out? Now? When I'm being accused of things I didn't do?"

"I just can't do this. Not right now. I need time to think."

"Jenna, please. Don't let this—don't let her—get between us."

"It's too late," I said.

He pressed his palms against the counter, breathing hard. "The timing, Jenna. God, the timing couldn't be worse. Emily said—"

"Oh my God." I laughed bitterly. "Are you seriously turning this into a legal strategy? You're worried about optics while our marriage is falling apart?"

His bravado faded. "Okay. I'll stay at the condo in the city," he said finally.

I didn't answer.

Braden grabbed his jacket, his keys, and the briefcase. He didn't bother to pack a bag. At the door, he turned back. "I didn't cheat on you, Jenna."

My laptop screen was still open on the video clip—paused on Heather's face as she glanced up at the camera, mouth slightly agape. I didn't look at him.

The door clicked shut. The house went silent, until I burst into tears.

I had never felt so alone.

FOURTEEN

I woke up to the sound of my phone vibrating on the nightstand. I reached for Braden out of instinct, forgetting for a moment that he was gone. That I had kicked him out of the house. My hand found the phone.

It was a text from Madison. I was heading over there in an hour to pick up Lucy.

But she hadn't texted me about that. I wasn't sure what she was texting about, so I read it again.

Madison: *You see this? Call me.*

Before I could reply, she sent another text with a link. I could tell from the link preview that it was to the *Tech Truth Unfiltered* website.

My stomach sank.

TTU was a tech tabloid site. One of the most popular tech focused news sites in the Bay Area. It focused more on the salacious than on actual business news coverage. Millionaire and billionaire techies gone bad.

I hesitated, already knowing this was going to hurt. But I clicked anyway.

The headline hit me like a punch.

BIOTECH DARLING HUDSON TITAN'S $1.2B MERGER IMPLODES — SEX, LIES, AND A BLOWN DEAL.

Langford, Hayes & Fox, one of the top law firms in the state, finds itself in hot water thanks to one of its senior partners, Braden Morrissey. Not only was he in charge of the blown merger deal that caused the prestigious firm to be fired by Hudson Titan, its former billion-dollar blue-chip client, but Mr. Morrissey has also been accused of sexual shenanigans! Court filings reviewed by TTU reveal that Morrissey, 43, has been accused of inappropriate conduct by a subordinate employee, Heather Evans.

Evans, 23, who was Mr. Morrissey's paralegal, claims Morrissey, who is married with a young child, created a hostile work environment after she ended their three-month affair. The hoity-toity law firm refused to comment on the blown deal, and their paralegals' lawsuit, but they did confirm that the firm terminated Morrissey last week. Court documents show that a temporary restraining order has been issued, barring Mr. Morrissey from contacting his former paralegal/lover.

Documents obtained by TTU also reveal that the merger—already months behind schedule—collapsed after "critical mismanagement" on Morrissey's part. To make things even juicier here in the Bay, the alleged lecher, Braden Morrissey is scion of THE Morrissey family, one of the richest and most famous old-money lumber families in San Francisco, with deep roots and significant influence in the city. The accused frisky and incompetent attorney's great grandfather was a former mayor of The City. Sources within the firm describe him as "entitled" and "checked out." One added, "He's a trust-fund kid who's never faced consequences. Well, it seems the party is over for the rich legal bro.

Attached beneath the article was *the photograph*—Braden and Heather at Niza Café.

I felt like I'd been punched again, harder this time. The comments section was already bustling with typical cruelty, empowered by the anonymity of social media, where everyone has an opinion they think is worth sharing, not caring that there are real people involved—including an innocent eleven-year-old child. My eyes began to tear again as I read the comments thinking about Lucy.

He looks exactly like the type.

Another rich asshole abusing his power.

Hope she sues him for everything he's got.

A Chad being a Chad. Shocker.

There was a smaller photo below it—our house. Our *house.* Cropped from the real estate listing from five years ago. The caption read:

"Morrissey and his wife, Jenna Morrissey, reside in the uber affluent Vista Bay neighborhood of Marin County."

Seeing my name printed there—*Jenna Morrissey*—felt like being stripped in public. The whole world suddenly had access to our address, our marriage, our shame.

I felt the blood drain from my face.

The author of this garbage article was Ted Hook. His profile picture sat there smugly beside the byline. Crew cut, platinum bleached blond hair. The Slim-Shady look with a contemptuous smirk plastered on his face. His bio read:

"Ted Hook is the love child of John Carreyrou and Perez Hilton. He brings you the scandals the Valley doesn't want you to know. Tips welcomed. Your anonymity is assured!"

Perfect.

My hands shook as I scrolled. He'd tagged Braden's LinkedIn profile, the firm's official page, and half the tech CEOs who had once toasted Braden at firm events and swanky parties.

A notification banner slid across my screen from Madison: *Sorry! But you're trending.*

For a second, I couldn't breathe.

I checked the comments on my last Instagram post— me and Lucy at Stinson Beach two weekends ago.

The internet mob had slithered on over to my account.

How could you marry such a creep!

I guess being a trophy wife isn't what it's cracked up to be lol.

Poor kid. Hope she never dates anyone like her scumbag dad in the future.

Money can't buy morals.

Do your child a favor. Kill yourself you worthless gold digger.

KYS was posted over and over.

I stopped. How could people be so nasty? Wishing me harm like that.

After setting my account to private and disabling comments, I shut the app. I didn't even dare going to Twitter or Reddit.

I sat there on the kitchen island stunned.

The house felt different now. Smaller, darker. Even the walls seemed to recoil from the shame of being associated with us.

A call came through. It was Braden. I let it ring until it stopped. Then his voicemail:

"Jenna, don't read that trash. My lawyer's handling it. They're going to send a cease-and-desist. She's getting us a PR crisis team. But for now, don't engage, don't post, don't reply to comments, don't talk to anyone. Especially reporters. I know you don't want to talk to me, but we need to talk now. Please call me back."

I didn't even know what to do. Because it wasn't just *his* reputation that was ruined now. It was mine. Lucy's. Oh God. There was no way to keep her in the dark now about what had been going on.

And I knew the gossip cycle—once it starts, it doesn't stop. Not in Marin, not in the Bay, not anywhere, especially online.

The downfall of a rich Marin couple generated clicks and views for content creators. I knew this was just the beginning of that online harassment.

The kettle on the stove started a shrill and piercing whistle. I had forgotten that I had set it.

I shut it off and stood there, staring out at the bay. And my skin crawled. It felt like the city was staring back at me. The entire San Francisco skyline gawking and snickering at us.

Then my phone began to ping nonstop. One notification after another, after another. I didn't recognize any of them. I put my phone on silent mode. If it wasn't for Lucy, I would have tossed the damned thing into the ocean.

I had to get Lucy at Madison's. I didn't want her to find out about this from assholes online.

Grabbing my keys, I ran out the door. My hands shook on the steering wheel as I backed out of the driveway.

Madison's house was only six minutes away, but every four-way stop sign felt like punishment.

I kept seeing Lucy's face in my head as she scrolled on her phone, her friends whispering. My baby reading those nasty comments about her parents. About her.

Then a new panic hit: What if reporters or those online sleuths started digging into my past? The one thing I'd buried so deep I'd convinced myself it was gone forever. I wanted to pull over and throw up, but I had just turned onto Madison's street. My pulse hurt from racing hard. All I wanted to do right now was to get to my child, hold her tightly, and protect her.

I expected a throng of paparazzi; thankfully, there was no one. I felt a sense of relief. In the scale of things, we were nobodies, so hopefully this post wouldn't have long legs and wouldn't bleed off the internet into our real lives.

Madison's neighborhood was quiet except for the whirring of leaf blowers and the distant bark of a dog. Perfectly normal morning for everyone else.

Once I parked crookedly at the curb, I half ran up the walkway. Madison opened the door before I knocked.

"Jenna," she said softly. She looked like she'd been expecting me. "I was just about to call."

"Has she seen it?" I asked, breathless.

Madison shook her head. "No. Not yet. I've kept her away from the internet. But..." She hesitated. "My husband mentioned it at breakfast. It's everywhere."

I pressed a hand to my mouth. The bile rose hot.

"Lucy's in the kitchen," Madison said quietly. "She just finished breakfast. Pancakes."

I forced myself to walk, not run. Lucy was sitting at the island finishing breakfast. She was in a deep conversation with Chase about Pokemon. She looked up, bright and innocent.

"Mom! You're early. Did Dad call? Are we going home?"

Her voice cracked me open.

"Yeah, sweetheart," I said. "We're going home." I brushed a strand of hair from her cheek and tried to smile. "Say thank you to Mrs. Taylor, okay?"

Madison caught my eye over Lucy's head with that look of pity people give when they know something awful and don't know what to do with it.

Lucy slipped her backpack on, chattering about pancakes and video games, oblivious to the firestorm that had settled over our family.

My phone kept trilling, each burst like nails on a chalkboard. As we walked to the car, she said, "Mom, why is your phone blowing up?"

"Telemarketers," I lied.

She gave me a look of pure disbelief.

We buckled in. I managed a thin smile as I started the car. A moment later I was driving back to the house, wondering how long until some kid mentioned it at school? Until she heard her father's name paired with *sexual harassment* and *lawsuit?* Until she realized we were now news fodder.

If my past was going to get exposed, I needed to get ahead of it first.

I pressed harder on the gas, as if I could outrun the internet.

FIFTEEN

I'D HOPED THE *TECH TRUTH UNFILTERED* ARTICLE would sink to the bottom of their site by lunchtime. Instead, by mid-morning it was trending and had been picked up by the mainstream news sites like MSNBC, Fox News, and CNN.

The implosion of a billion-dollar deal Wall Street had been salivating over—plus the hint of a sex scandal—was catnip for a slow news day.

By late afternoon, the media world had set up camp in my life.

The doorbell started ringing and it wouldn't stop.

At first, I thought it was a delivery. But it wasn't.

Reporters.

A couple of them milled about at the end of our driveway, but one woman walked right up to our front door. Her hair was perfectly curled and she was holding a mic. A cameraman followed, the lens already pointed toward the house. She didn't bother with the doorbell; she knocked on the door, making Sunny lose it as he barked at the intruder.

"Mrs. Morrissey! Jenna! Do you have a comment about your husband's relationship with Heather Evans?"

I cracked the door open, hiding behind it. "No comment. Get off my property or I'm calling the police." I slammed the door in her face. That actually felt pretty good.

When I turned around, Lucy was standing there, calming down Sunny.

"Mom, what's going on? Why are there people outside?"

My smile felt stapled on. "Nothing, sweetheart. Just... people from the news. Wrong house."

I hit the remote to drop every shade in the house, even the ones out back towards the bay, though there was a steep hillside and a plunge down into the waters on that side.

The phone started buzzing again — numbers I didn't recognize. Unknowns. Local. Out of state.

Although I turned it face down, it kept vibrating against the counter like a trapped bee.

By noon, the story had gone from local gossip to national clickbait. Every aggregator site picked it up. Hashtags spread—#MorrisseyMergerFail, #HeatherEvans, #TrustFundPredator.

The companies involved in the failed merger issued curt *no comment* statements while the firm distanced itself even further from Braden, reminding everyone "Mr. Morrissey was terminated." Even the *San Francisco Chronicle* had a developing banner on its homepage about Braden's legal woes.

I tried to shield Lucy away from it all. I took her phone away, which upset her to no end.

It was a futile gesture. Every second of Lucy's young life had been tethered to the Internet, and although I was taken aback, I wasn't surprised when she showed me the *TTU* article pulled up on her Nintendo Switch device. I had no idea you could access the Internet on those things. Of course she'd found a way. Kids always do.

I should have unplugged the Wi-Fi router. I wasn't mad at her; I was actually impressed. Besides, nothing good comes from lies and secrets. I knew that better than most.

"Mom, why is everyone talking about Dad?"

"People say things online that aren't true," I said softly. "You know that, right?"

She frowned. "One of my friends told me I shouldn't go on TikTok."

My throat tightened.

"I don't want you online today," I said, more sharply than I meant to. "Promise me."

Lucy nodded, wide-eyed. "Okay."

A knock at the door made us jump.

This time it wasn't the reporters. It was Nina from next door, holding her yoga mat like a peace offering. So I let her in, though I couldn't remember the last time she had come over, if ever.

"I just wanted to check on you," she said, words dripping with curiosity masked as concern. "I can't believe what's being said online. You must be mortified."

I bit the inside of my cheek to keep from screaming. "We're fine, Nina. Thanks for checking."

She hesitated, searching for more gossip to take back to her group chat. When she realized I wasn't giving her any, she gave a too-broad smile and left.

I locked the door behind her and leaned against it, breathing shallowly. Through the slats of the blinds, I saw her on the curb talking to a reporter. Great.

The hours blurred after that—calls, texts, notifications stacking like bricks. By two o'clock, Braden's name was trending worldwide.

By three, even my old college roommate, someone I hadn't spoken to in over a decade, texted: *"Holy crap. Is that your husband?"*

At four, my phone vibrated again. Braden.

I almost didn't answer. Lucy was on the couch watching *The Great British Baking Show*, Sunny curled at her feet. Braden had texted earlier, asking to see her. And Lucy kept asking where her dad was.

She looked so small, so normal, so innocent.

I answered.

"Jenna. Please," he said hoarsely. "I just want to see her. I'll use the side gate. I'll be in and out, no one will see me."

Every instinct screamed no — but Lucy deserved to see her father.

"Fine," I said quietly.

He arrived at dusk.

Brendan had parked down at the ferry lot, rented an e-bike, and pedaled the two-mile climb to our house. When I saw him through the patio doors—Giants cap pulled low, sunglasses on, shoulders tense—I barely recognized him.

Was this what our lives had devolved to?

When I opened the doors, he slipped inside without a word. He looked exhausted and frayed around the edges, but he still carried that faint Morrissey confidence like a reflex he couldn't shut off.

"Where is she?" he asked.

"In the living room."

He didn't wait.

Lucy looked up when he entered and froze for half a beat — then she launched herself off the couch and into his arms. "Daddy!"

He caught her and held her close. "Hey, chickadee. Oh man, I missed you."

She clung to him. "Everyone is talking about you. They're saying mean stuff."

"I know," he said softly, kissing her hair. "People say things that aren't true sometimes. But you know your dad, right?"

Lucy nodded into his chest. "I told them they were liars."

Something in his face cracked—a mixture of pride and devastation.

I stood by the doorway, arms crossed, watching. I didn't want to interrupt. I didn't want to feel anything at all, but it hurt.

He stayed with her for almost half an hour. They played with Sunny in the backyard, tossed a tennis ball around, and for a brief, fragile stretch of time, it looked like any other day.

When Lucy went upstairs to shower, Braden came back into the kitchen. The light was low and golden, spilling across the counter where the morning's untouched coffee still sat cold.

"I want to come home," he said quietly.

"You can't," I said without looking up.

"Jenna, please. This—being away—it's unbearable. I need to be here. For you. For her."

I turned to face him. "Braden, it's been twenty-four hours since the world found out every ugly detail of our lives. Reporters were outside. I'm being called a gold-digging whore online. Our daughter's classmates are whispering about her father. You think I can just... pretend that isn't happening?"

He swallowed hard. "I just need a chance to make it right."

"I need time," I said. "That's all I know."

Deflated, he nodded slowly. "Okay. I can give you that." He hesitated, then added, "I'm sorry, Jenna. For all of it. For what I've put you and Lucy through."

The apology was soft, genuine, but it couldn't reach me. Not yet.

"I know," I said finally. "But sorry doesn't erase what's been done."

Eyes glossy, he reached for his jacket. "I'll go." At the patio doors, he paused. "Tell Lucy I'll call her tomorrow?"

"I will."

He lingered, like he wanted to say more but didn't.

Then he left.

I watched him walk across the backyard and slip out the back gate.

Sunny padded over, leaning his head against my leg, trying to cheer me up.

Beneath the shame and anger I felt towards Braden, a deeper fear twisted in me: What if my secret from all those years ago got dragged into this mess too?

SIXTEEN

I HAD BEEN LOCKED UP FOR ALMOST THREE YEARS. Soon I would be free. And that day couldn't come fast enough.

I shouldn't complain. Killers like myself are usually locked up for life. In some parts of the country, they put down murderers. But that was not my fate. I had three things in my favor. One, I was only fifteen when I killed my foster father. That skidmark. Two, he was a pedo. No one likes those fucking degenerates. Even in prison, they're bottom rung on the incarcerated food chain. Permanent greenlight to take them out at will. Three, I had the juvenile corrections system eating out of the palm of my hand.

Those idiots were proud of themselves for the bang-up job rehabilitating me. The state was just covering its ass for putting a child in the care of a predator. And I was playing that card beautifully.

Every shrink report said I was making progress.

That was the word they used—progress.

Like I was some kind of science project inching toward a result they could hang their hat on.

By seventeen, I knew the system better than most of the guards did. I knew what words got you privileges, that tears got you sympathy, and silences made them nervous enough to give me whatever I wanted. Well, not everything I wanted. I was still locked up.

Every Wednesday morning was group therapy. A half-circle of plastic chairs, a whiteboard with phrases like *accountability* and *healing through honesty*. The counselor, Ms. Ortega, was nice enough. She wanted to believe we could all be saved. That was her mistake.

The other girls sat slumped in their chairs, arms crossed, eyes dead. They'd learned that talking too much only gave other inmates something to use against you. I talked just enough to benefit me.

"I think about that night every day," I'd say softly, eyes down. "I wish I could take it back. I really do."

Cue the lip tremble, the chin quiver, and—six seconds later—tears. Real ones. Well, *real enough*.

The counselor nodded, murmuring encouragement, scribbling notes.

Inside, I was laughing.

It was an asinine conversation. I couldn't take it back. Full stop. But, if I lived in this pseudoscience fantasy world of theirs, I wouldn't take it back. I would have shot him twice.

They thought I was healing. I was rehearsing.

The chaplain came by on Thursdays. He was older, kind, a retired priest, always smelling of coffee and Bengay. He said forgiveness was possible for everyone, even a murderer like me. I memorized his favorite Bible verses and repeated them back to him the next week, word for word. He started calling me "his little redemption story."

That title got me an extra phone call and a pass to the outdoor garden twice a week. Worth every Amen.

In everything I did, I reminded them that I was a victim. And I was, but I wasn't going to let that define me. I had already passed beyond that night, but I wouldn't let the authorities know that.

I pretended to study hard to earn my GED when it was so easy I could have aced it with my eyes closed. But by pretending to overcome a dyslexia I never had, I got the volunteer teachers to enthusiastically give me—and, in turn, themselves—pats on the back and fist bumps. God, I hated fist bumps. But I enthusiastically returned the gesture every time.

Six months ago, they'd given me an IQ test, and they were enthralled at my score: 136. An IQ of 130 or higher was classified as "very superior" or "gifted."

I knew I was smart, especially compared to the space cadets that were locked up with me.

But not all my fellow inmates were useless to me. In fact, the person who really taught me something useful in prison was Monalisa Guerra.

She was an East LA proud chola. We were the same height and body types. Except for her brown skin contrasting with my milky-white complexion, we could pass for sisters.

Her brown hair was cropped short, GI-Jane style; I kept mine shoulder-length. I played up my girly attractive features, as it was currency in there; Monalisa tried to hide that she was conventionally beautiful, like me. I figured that was why she always scowled with a stare that could cut glass.

There was something ambiguous about her—part girl, part warrior—and she ruled our cell block like a warden behind the walls. The guards respected her. The other inmates feared her. No one messed with her.

She took an interest in me early on. Said I had "potential." That was her word for it. She saw through the bullshit act that had staff fooled, and she loved it. She had given me my prison nickname: Meryl. As in Meryl Streep, one of the greatest actors ever.

"You got that pretty face and that smart mouth," she told me. "You learn how to use 'em right and nobody can touch you."

And she meant it literally.

Once Monalisa took me under her wing, and I became

her roomie, I was untouchable. No one messed with her girls. And I was her favorite.

At night, when the lights dimmed and the guards did their rounds, I'd lie next to her in that narrow bunk, and I'd let her hands wander about my body, kissing her back passionately. For me, it wasn't love. I wasn't confused about my sexuality, I knew I was straight. It was survival.

But most importantly, unlike my pig of a foster father, I let Monalisa do those things. She never took me by force, like he had. She got what she wanted, and I got what I wanted.

Monalisa protected what was hers. I gave her loyalty, attention, and warmth. The currency she craved.

Beyond giving me her protection, she taught me things that mattered more than any retired priest regurgitating passages from a 2,000-year-old book or any psychobabble from a poorly paid prison psychologist.

Monalisa taught me how to read people. How to hustle.

How to find their weak spots. Fellow inmates. Guards. Staff.

How to play people without them even realizing they'd been played.

She'd lean close, whispering about valuable skills for me once I got outside. How to steal an identity. How to get fake IDs. Open a fake bank account. About carding and crypto scams.

She called it "the hustle."

The counselors thought I was rehabilitating.

But every night, with Monalisa's arm around me and her raspy voice in my ear, I was learning the real lessons on how the real world worked.

She used men, mostly. She said they were the easiest marks. "They see what they want to see," she'd laugh. "You cry a little, look scared, and they'll hand you their wallet, their heart, and their soul."

I soaked up every word.

They all thought I was just another broken foster kid waiting for redemption. But I wasn't broken. And I didn't want their pity. I was learning how to win.

When my defense attorney showed up with that plea deal, I knew the show had worked. The shrink wrote glowing reports about my remorse. The chaplain vouched for my soul. Even the warden said I had "promise" and was worth "saving."

"Plead guilty to involuntary manslaughter," my lawyer said. "You'll be out at eighteen."

My record would be sealed. I would get out with a clean slate.

He smiled, knowing he was giving me a second chance few of his clients ever get. I smiled because I had played them all.

Monalisa laughed. "Three years for killing a dude. Goddamn, Meryl, you're the GOAT around here!"

The system thought they were saving me after I'd messed up so badly.

But the truth was, I didn't need saving.

I'd learned something far more useful: It's easier to manipulate the system than to fight it.

And from that moment, that became the plan.

Because once I got out, I wasn't going back to being poor. I'd spent my whole life hungry; hungry for food, for safety, for control. I wasn't going to start over just to end up broke and forgotten in some trailer park on food stamps.

No, I'd use what I had. My brains, my looks, my charm, to make sure I never went without again.

I had big plans once I got out. And they went beyond the social workers' wet dream of rehabilitation. I was already working on a different kind of recovery—financial security.

They said my life could be salvaged and that I could have a bright future after I was released.

I couldn't have agreed more. But I wasn't going to play by their rules. I was going to take what I wanted.

SEVENTEEN

Another night in the condo, alone. My unwanted bachelor pad. The Giants were playing the Diamondbacks on TV, but I could care less. I just needed the noise. Silence was worse. It left too much room for thinking.

I was on my fourth bourbon. I knew I'd been drinking too much; I wasn't clueless. But it was the only way to dull the sound of my own failure.

I stood, feeling woozy. I looked out the window. I was on the 34th floor of what used to be my bachelor pad—a gift from my parents after graduating from college. Once Jenna and I got serious, she moved in here with me. Once Lucy was born, we both felt that raising a child on the other side of the bridge was more to our liking. But we kept the condo. It was fully paid. A good investment. And I worked in the city, so it was nice to have a place a little closer to work.

The memory of work made me queasy. I was sure it was that and not the booze.

The city stretched out beneath me through the floor-to-ceiling windows—glass towers, blinking lights and, somewhere down there, my name splattered across every news feed, every gossip site, iPads, every damned phone for anyone curious enough to click.

Fucking Ted Hook. I wanted to sue him and *TTU* into oblivion, but Emily advised against it. Tabloids are like a bad, itchy rash. No matter how badly you want to scratch it, it's best to leave it alone. It will eventually go away. The more you mess with the itch, the worse it gets.

I liked the analogy. Ted Hook was like a bad rash on mankind. I laughed at the thought.

As I looked down, the dark whispering in my head started again like when I was on the ledge of the ferry: *Just step out the window and it's over.* Instead, I stepped back, terrified of my own thoughts.

Turning back towards the kitchen, I topped off my drink and took a long gulp. The warmth in my stomach felt good, but I started to cough as the bourbon burned my throat.

I missed Jenna. I missed Lucy. I missed my old life. How could I have messed up our lives this bad? It seemed unreal. This had to be some sort of horrible nightmare I couldn't wake up from. But it wasn't. It was all too real. All because of her.

I needed to get out. I needed to be around people. So I grabbed my jacket and I headed outside towards the elevator.

As I walked through the lobby, I thought I was fine, but the security guard asked me, "Are you okay, Mr. Morrissey? You seem a bit unsteady there. Should I help you back to your condo, sir?" A not-so-subtle hint.

"No, thank you, Fred. I'm fine, just going for a walk. I need fresh air." I noticed I slurred my words a bit there too.

In my head, I ran a tally. *How many drinks have I had tonight? Two? No, more than that. Five? Ah, I'm fine.* I walked outside and the cool night air felt good. I started moving down Folsom Street towards Joe D. one of the last old-school dive bars left in the city, on First Street. This wasn't a trendy faux dive bar, it was the real deal. Been here for decades. Probably wouldn't last too long, as every old haunt in San Francisco eventually became gentrified. Bars included.

The floor was sticky. It was crowded, but not too packed. Hypnotic sitars waft from the speakers as Tom Petty's "Don't Come Around Here No More" starts booming.

I snagged a stool near the end and ordered a shot of Jameson and a beer back. The first went down like fire, the second like regret. By the third round, the noise in my head quieted. In fact, the whole place seemed out of focus.

Until I looked up at the giant mirror behind the bar and I saw her. At first I thought it was the booze. So I turned around. No, it was her. Heather walked in.

She sauntered in like she owned the place, without a care in the world. She wore a long, green, quilted barn jacket. Black sacks. Red loafers. Her hair was perfectly coiffed. A faint smirk on her ruby-red painted lips. She was being loud; her voice rang in my ears and sounded like nails on a chalkboard.

And she wasn't alone. I recognized the guy she was with. It took me a second, but then I placed him: Ryan Kim, one of the paralegals from the firm.

She saw me before I could look away. For a second, our eyes locked. Her smile faltered. Then she turned sharply, said something to Ryan, and headed for the door.

I don't remember standing. I don't remember paying the bar tab. One minute I was on the stool, the next I was outside, the cold night air slapping me sober, or trying to.

She was walking away from me. "Heather!" I yelled.

Heather froze. The noise of the street seemed to fade around us. She turned around, her eyes wide and trembling. Ryan turned, stepping in front of her as if he were protecting her. From whom? Me? I felt an anger that scared me. But I didn't care. I stepped towards them. Ryan held out his hand.

"Braden, don't," he said.

I moved closer. "You lying bitch," I spat before I could stop myself. "You ruined my life. Why? Why would you do this to me?"

Heather shrank behind Ryan, eyes wider, trembling like a scared little girl. "Please, just go," she said. "You're not supposed to be near me."

That word hit me like a punch. Near. The TRO which even in my inebriated state, I knew I was violating.

"Don't you dare pull that act," I said. "You know this is bullshit. You set me up!"

"Hey!" Ryan stepped forward, both palms out. "You need to back off, man."

I could feel eyes on us; gawkers on the sidewalk, excited for some action, phones rising. Recording. Always recording. We can't have a goddamned second of privacy anymore. I knew I should walk away, but I seemed unable to. Like my logic and good sense had been disabled.

I took another step closer, shouting, "You're not going to get away with this!" I felt hands on my chest shoving me back. It was Ryan. Not hard, but enough to warn me. But something in me snapped. I lunged.

And that's when his fist connected with my face.

White light as pain bloomed across my cheekbone.

I fell back and landed on my butt.

I hit the pavement hard, my palms scraping the dirty sidewalk. Someone shouted. A woman screamed.

I blinked up at the streetlights, disoriented, tasting blood. My ears rang.

Heather was crying now—loud, theatrical sobs. I caught words between them: "Former boss... attacked me... TRO..."

Ryan had an arm around her as he glared down at me.

A patrol car chirped at the curb. Blue-and-red lights washed the sidewalk and my throbbing cheek. I looked up; my right eye was already swelling. Two uniforms climbed out of the black-and-white—young, stone-faced, hands resting on their duty belts like they'd done this a thousand times.

"What's going on here?" one asked.

"He came after her," Ryan said immediately. "He's her former boss. There's a restraining order which he violated."

The words blurred together, like I was underwater. I tried to speak, but everything came out slurred. "She—set—me—up—"

One cop knelt beside me. "Sir, have you been drinking tonight?"

I laughed, because even in my condition I knew it was such a stupid question. What could I say? No? I'm a lawyer, I knew I should have kept my mouth shut. But I didn't. "Yeah. So what? It's not a crime, is it?"

"It can be when you're bothering people and acting like a fool in public," the police officer said curtly. "Come on, get up," he added, making me realize I was still sitting on the sidewalk.

He grabbed my arm and helped me to my feet. I was about to thank him when he twisted it behind my back. The metal cuffs bit into my wrists.

"You're under arrest for public intoxication, disorderly conduct, and violation of a restraining order."

"You don't understand," I muttered, struggling. "She's lying. She's lying!"

Heather watched from behind Ryan, tears and black mascara streaking her cheeks, her lower lip trembling. The look of horror in her face made me do a double-take. Am I the monster here?

As the cops walked me to the car, some tech bro in an Oxford shirt yelled, "Hey, isn't that the guy from the article?"

I heard someone else yell out: "Yeah, Morrissey."

Phones everywhere. Screens glowing like judgment. A humiliating perp walk from the curb to the patrol car.

They pushed me into the backseat, lowering my head to avoid me banging it. Then the door slammed shut.

Through the glass, I saw Heather hugging Ryan, her face buried in his shoulder. Then she glanced up and looked around. Ryan was facing the officers, who took his statement. Just for a second or two, she looked at me, and she winked. Immediately after, she buried her face back into Ryan's shoulder, sobbing.

I started shouting. "Did you see that? She's fucking lying. That bitch is lying!"

"Shut up!" was the response I got from the officer as the car started moving and I stared out at the blur of neon and headlights. My reflection looked nothing like me— blood on my chin, eyes glassy, disheveled.

I didn't even know what I'd done wrong anymore.

All I knew was she'd won.

EIGHTEEN

THE PHONE RANG BEFORE SUNRISE.

That alone was enough to make my stomach clench. No one calls at six a.m. with good news. I glanced at Braden's side of the bed out of instinct. Empty. It still startled me, even after everything.

For a moment, I thought something had happened to Lucy. My heart dropped before I even looked at the screen. But I remembered she was fast asleep with Sunny in her bedroom. I looked at the screen, wiping the sleep from my eyes.

It was Emily Acosta.

I hesitated before answering. I certainly wasn't her favorite person since I hadn't attended Braden's first meeting with her. One of her associates had left me a message a couple days ago, saying they needed to talk to me as they prepared Braden's defense. But I was not ready to deal with it, so I hadn't returned their call.

Calling me at this hour seemed inappropriate. My hand shook slightly as I swiped to pick up.

"Yes," I said, coldly.

"Am I speaking to Jenna Morrissey?"

"Why are you calling me at six a.m., and waking me up?"

"Ms. Morrissey," she said, brisk and professional. "I'm afraid there's been an incident."

I already knew. Not the details, just the feeling. That quiet, cold recognition that something else had cracked, which was why she would call me at this time.

"What kind of incident?" I asked.

"Your husband was taken into custody last night in San Francisco."

I closed my eyes. "Custody? You mean, arrested?"

"Yes, Braden was arrested last night by the SFPD."

Now I was sitting on the edge of my bed. The morning chill suddenly had more bite than usual.

"Braden? Arrested? For what?"

"Violation of the TRO, simple assault, disorderly conduct and public intoxication."

None of that made any sense. Did she dial the wrong client?

"What?" is all I managed to say.

Emily sighed. "He apparently encountered Ms. Evans at a bar and—" She hesitated. "There was an altercation."

For a few seconds, the words didn't register. They just hung there like a stubborn dark cloud.

Then her words landed, one by one, each heavier than the last.

"Heather?" I said. "You're telling me he saw Heather?"

"Yes. Police responded to a disturbance outside a bar. There were witnesses. Ms. Evans claimed he approached her aggressively."

I got out of bed but felt woozy; I gripped the night stand to steady myself. "Oh, God. How did this happen?"

"He went to Joe D.'s bar for a drink," Emily said.

Of course he was drinking, I thought, getting angry at him again.

"It appears it was a random encounter. Ms. Evans was on a date. She walked in while he was there. When she saw him, she left, but he followed her outside and began to berate her. Allegedly, he was aggressive towards her, and the male companion with Ms. Evans had to get physical to get Braden to stop lunging at her."

"He attacked her?" I couldn't believe he would do that.

"No, thank God, he didn't touch her. But moved her towards her aggressively. So Ms. Evan's date got physical.

"Physical? How?"

"He punched Braden."

This couldn't be real. I'd never seen Braden being

aggressive towards anyone. I didn't think he'd been in a fight his whole life. Now he was mixed up in a street fight.

"Is he okay?" I asked finally. My voice sounded strange and flat, detached.

"He's okay, all things considered. Physically fine. Emotionally... that's another story. We're working on bail right now. I'll have him home in a few hours."

"Well, thanks for letting me know," I mumbled, unsure of what to do or say.

"I'll let you know when we bail him out."

"Right," I murmured. "Thank you for calling."

"Of course. I'll be in touch later today."

When the line went dead, I realized I'd been gripping the phone so hard my fingers had gone numb. I set it down and pressed my palms to my face.

A sob tried to claw its way up my throat, but I forced it back down. I was too tired for tears.

Lucy was still asleep, thank God. I walked through the quiet house. The morning light filtered weakly through the half-closed blinds, and I felt like I was drifting through someone else's life.

I went to the kitchen and made coffee. On the island there was not food, but the stack of papers from the lawsuit I had copied.

My phone pinged again. This time, it wasn't Emily.

It was Madison. Her text message: *I'm so sorry*. And a link to a tweet from Ted Hook.

I didn't want to look, but I did.

Disgraced attorney Braden Morrissey was arrested after violating a restraining order and attacking his ex-lover at a SOMA bar.

Then my heart sank even lower. Hook had a video from someone's phone of Braden being escorted into the patrol car, his face pale and bloody, a flash of fear and anger caught mid-frame.

I covered my mouth with my hand.

Oh God. It was already everywhere.

My phone pinged again, and again, messages from people I knew, and from numbers I didn't recognize.

Thinking of you.

So sorry, hun. What a mess.

Is it true he hit her?

I put the phone face down. I couldn't read another word.

When Lucy woke up, I tried to keep my voice steady. She came into the kitchen rubbing her eyes, her hair a mess.

"Morning, Mom."

"Hey, sweetheart," I said, forcing a smile. "Are you hungry?"

She nodded, sitting at the counter while I scrambled eggs with shaking hands.

I tried to act normal by making her breakfast, packing her lunch, talking about the weather, anything to keep her away from the online world for a little longer.

But I kept glancing at the clock, waiting for Braden to call, for the next explosion to go off.

I drove Lucy to school. Cara and her clique of mean-girl moms looked at me with thin smiles. I could tell by the way the glee in their eyes they knew about Braden's arrest. My chest tightened.

I WAS WALKING through the front door after the drop off, and the embarrassment from the other Marin moms, when my phone buzzed. It was Braden.

"Jenna," he said quietly. He sounded hoarse, defeated. "I'm sorry."

I almost hung up right then.

"I made everything worse. I was at the bar, and she walked in, and I just lost it. I didn't plan it. I swear to God I didn't. I just… snapped. And then she—"

"You were drunk," I said, cutting him off.

He breathed for a moment before he spoke.

"I know. It's gotten out of control. I'm going to deal with that. With everything. I promise."

I didn't know how to respond.

Braden sighed. "She set me up, Jenna. You have to believe me."

"I don't know what to believe anymore."

There was more silence on the other end. Long, heavy silence.

"I'm not a monster," he said finally. "No matter what it looks like."

Again, I didn't answer. Because I wasn't sure if I still knew who he was.

"Please," he said softly. "Don't give up on me."

Before I could start crying again, I hung up.

The sunlight pooled across the kitchen floor and I stood staring at it. My whole body felt like it was shaking, some awful vibration I couldn't shut off.

Outside, an Amazon delivery van rumbled by. The world kept moving. People went to work. Kids went to school. And I was standing in my kitchen, waiting for the next headline to destroy whatever was left of us.

NINETEEN

Two days after Braden's arrest, there were multiple videos from different angles of Braden berating Heather then lunging towards her, and Ryan's punch followed by Braden falling on his ass. They were everywhere online. Someone had edited a super cut of the confrontation and his arrest into one video.

It had gone viral within hours. I don't know where it was posted first, but it had spread like a wildfire to X, TikTok, YouTube, Threads, Reddit, Fishbowl, even Nextdoor.

It was edited with cartoon sounds for the punch when he was hit, and the sound of Wiley Coyote falling as Braden hit the ground. Another person added the *Cops* theme "Bad Boys" as he was arrested and shoved into the police car.

People added captions, filters, stitches, reaction videos.

"Fallen Tech Bro Lawyer Meltdown."

"Karma's a Bitch Rich Boy."

"Trust Fund Predator Gets Decked. Love it!"

By the next morning, video screen grabs of Braden's bloody face had become meme currency. San Francisco had stopped releasing official mug shots to the public a few years ago, if not, I'm sure that would be plastered all over the place. But it didn't matter. There was more than enough content to keep the masses happy.

Online they loved it. The schadenfreude of watching a rich, successful man fall apart in 4K was manna from heaven.

Braden Morrissey, once the golden boy of Bay Area law and member of the San Francisco elite, was now digital chum in the water. Everyone wanted a bite.

But as the internet does, it eventually moved on. The next scandal came, the next outrage.

Still, the damage was done.

In our world, silence didn't mean peace. It just meant people had gone on to whispering behind closed doors.

And, somehow, that felt worse.

Some random internet stranger's fifteen seconds of outrage could only sting for so long, but the quiet judgment of people in my real life? The stares, the smiles that weren't really smiles, the way conversations stopped when I walked into the room, those cut deeper.

Around Vista Bay, I felt like Hester Prynne: condemned by my own version of Puritan neighbors.

But sitting around the house sulking and hiding wasn't going to make this nightmare stop. I had to pull myself together and face it head-on.

I'd dealt with worse.

For too long, I'd been living inside this Marin County bubble, pretending comfort was the same as safety.

So when Emily Acosta asked for me and Braden to meet at her office downtown, I agreed.

When Braden texted to ask if we could grab coffee before the meeting, I surprised myself by saying yes.

We met at Philz Coffee, across the street from Emily's building in The Embarcadero. The place was crowded with tech workers in fleece vests and noise-canceling head-phones, each pretending to save the world one app, and one overpriced latte, at a time.

Braden was already there, sitting by the window.

He looked... smaller somehow. He had always imbued confidence and strength in the way he dressed and carried himself. But not now. In their place, slumped shoulders, a bluish-purple-black bruise under his right eye, and a half-hearted smile when he saw me.

He stood up awkwardly and waved. "Hey."

"Hey," I said back, walking over. He gestured to the table, where two large to-go cups sat waiting.

"I got your favorite—Jacob's Wonderbar with oat milk."

That almost made me smile. Almost.

"Thanks," I said, sitting down.

Something was painfully familiar about it. The way he'd already stirred the coffee for me, the napkin folded neatly by my cup. The small domestic gestures of a man who once had known me better than anyone. *Or thought he did.*

We'd been together for nineteen years. Married for fifteen.

You don't just erase that because everything went to hell.

I looked at him and felt my eyes watering, which I hated. I dabbed them with a napkin. "Sorry. I don't know why I'm—"

Braden shook his head. "No. Don't apologize. I know I sound like a broken record, but I'm truly sorry for everything I've put you and Lucy through."

For the first time in days, the anger in me softened.

"I know you are," I said quietly. Then, for reasons I couldn't explain, I started laughing. A small, nervous chuckle that surprised us both.

He raised an eyebrow. "What?"

I gestured at his face. "Boy, that dude really walloped you. That shiner's from one punch?"

His cheeks reddened. "I wasn't in the right state of mind, obviously."

"Obviously," I said, taking a sip of coffee. It was

perfect. A reminder that some things still worked the way they used to.

He looked out the window. "I know this doesn't mean much, since it's only been two days, but I stopped drinking."

That made me pause.

"You were right. It got out of control. Way before the bar. I guess it took a night in city jail to make me realize it."

I studied his face. The bruise, the tired eyes, the sincerity that felt fragile but real.

"That's... good," I said. "I'm glad to hear that, hon—" I stopped myself. "Braden."

He smiled faintly, then looked down. The silence between us was heavy but not hostile, like that of two people standing in the ashes of a house they once loved.

I changed the subject. "How was jail?"

He gave a humorless laugh. "Honestly? Terrifying at first. But not as bad as I expected. Once it hit me where I was... it was surreal. But no one messed with me. I guess I looked like every other idiot who made a bad decision after too many drinks. Emily got me out first thing in the morning."

"What did she say?"

"She tore into me." He grimaced. "Said she was close to dropping me as a client. But she didn't. Said she believes me." He wiped a tear away quickly, glancing around. "God, I'm so pathetic."

I shook my head. "You're not pathetic. You're human. And for what it's worth, I looked her up, you're in good hands. She's sharp."

He nodded. "She said we'll be fine, as long as I keep my head down. No interviews, that I should put myself under house arrest so I don't run into her again, nothing that can make me look even worse."

"After that night, that's a pretty low bar," I said, and we both chuckled softly. The kind of laugh that comes from exhaustion, not joy.

A pang of guilt hit me. If I hadn't kicked him out of the house in Vista Bay, he would've been home twenty miles from the city, and he would never have ended up at that bar where he ran into Heather. What were the odds?

For the next twenty minutes, we talked about Lucy. School. Her new art project. How Sunny had barked nonstop at reporters until I finally bribed him with treats. But finally, they had moved on, and getting to and from the house was pretty much back to normal.

Those few minutes felt... right. Like before. Like there was still a version of us that existed somewhere under all this wreckage.

When it was time to leave, he walked me to the corner, and the red light held us there.

He looked at me for a long time before saying, "I don't expect forgiveness. I just hope one day you'll see I wasn't the villain in all this."

"I never said you were the villain," I countered softly. "You just made some very bad choices."

His eyes shone with something that looked like regret. Or maybe love. Maybe both.

The light changed, and we crossed Drumm Street toward the Embarcadero Center. I looked up at the tower that housed Emily Acosta's office. It loomed above me, heavy and gray, but my fear was already morphing into something else. Anger. Not at Braden, at Heather Evans. All pretty and sweet, pretending to be the victim when she was a homewrecker.

It takes two to have an affair. I was ready to go on the offensive.

And that scared me.

TWENTY

EMILY ACOSTA'S OFFICE WAS A STATEMENT—A carefully curated testament to her success. The walls were a gallery of proof: photographs with A-list celebrities, from Hollywood stars to the Kardashians, to Ruth Bader Ginsburg and Michelle Obama. Another wall showcased her degrees and a constellation of legal awards.

I've always found it strange how lawyers display their credentials like art. You don't see accountants or engineers doing that. I never felt compelled to put up my BA degree on a wall. I don't even know where it is anymore.

Braden had done the same in his office. I wondered where his framed degrees had ended up—probably boxed and waiting to be shipped back to him by the firm.

I'd pictured Acosta's desk as one of those thick, old-school mahogany lawyer desks you see in movies, but it was the opposite—modern, almost surgical. An all-white

Herman Miller Renew, the kind that probably cost several thousand dollars, floating on slender die-cast aluminum legs. The surface was smooth and seamless, likely ash veneer over MDF, and at its center sat a single purple iMac like a jewel. The minimalist keyboard and wireless trackpad were spotless, so pristine they looked sterilized.

I felt like I should've wiped my shoes before walking in.

Behind her, a floor-to-ceiling window framed the city and the bay beyond. From this height, the cars crawling across the Bay Bridge looked like an ant trail—orderly, relentless, small.

Emily rose from behind her desk as we entered. She was tall, elegant, every movement deliberate. Her dark hair framed her face in a sleek, sculpted wave, not a strand out of place. Her suit—a tailored tweed jacket with a clean black trim—was the kind that whispered authority instead of shouting it. Simple, but precise. The kind of precision that came from knowing she didn't need to impress anyone; people already knew who she was.

Her makeup was impeccable—neutral tones, but with a slash of crimson lipstick that made her look both professional and dangerous. Her expression was calm, her eyes sharp, always appraising things.

If I hadn't known she was a lawyer, I might've guessed a surgeon, or maybe a CEO—the kind of woman who always controlled the room without raising her voice.

She extended a manicured hand, her gold Rolex Lady-Datejust watch catching the light. "Jenna. I'm glad you could make it."

Her tone wasn't warm, exactly, but it wasn't cold either. She sounded as if she had already decided she would win and expected everyone around her to keep up.

"Please, sit," she said, gesturing toward the two leather chairs in front of her immaculate white desk. Braden followed my lead, and we sat.

Emily remained standing for a moment, looking out the window toward the bay before turning back. "You've had a hell of a week," she said, her gaze flicking between us. "I won't sugarcoat this. The situation is serious. But..." She paused, the faintest smile curving her lips. "It's also starting to show cracks."

My stomach fluttered. "What kind of cracks?"

She sat down smoothly, crossing one leg over the other. "For one, Heather Evans's narrative isn't as airtight as her attorney wants everyone to believe. We've reviewed her HR complaint and her supporting evidence—the texts, the screenshots, the supposed timeline." She tapped a folder on her desk. "And already there are inconsistencies. Messages that appear to have been sent from Braden's phone when he was demonstrably in meetings with other people. Timestamps that don't align. Metadata that's been scrubbed or selectively preserved. And Braden's phone had gone missing."

I glanced at Braden. He looked as stunned as I felt. "You're saying she doctored evidence?" he asked.

"I'm saying it's a possibility," Emily replied. "And if she did, it's sloppy. Amateurish, even. Which tells me she's either reckless... or overconfident."

It seemed Heather had not thought that Braden would sic a pit bull of an attorney on the case. Braden believed this was all about setting up a Morrissey for a big pay day via a legal settlement. Make false claims, hire a lawyer to sue, then offer to settle quietly. There was an entire industry of lawyers in the racket. Lawyer shakedowns. Easy money if you target rich people who prefer to pay to make it go away. But Braden was fighting back.

I wasn't sure that was the case. For one, they hadn't thrown out a settlement number, at least not yet. If this was about money. Where was the offer to settle?

Emily smiled, pulling me from my thoughts. She leaned back slightly, folding her hands. "There's something else. Something I haven't shared with opposing counsel or even put in writing yet. My PI ran a background check on Heather Evans."

My pulse ticked up. "And?"

"She's practically a ghost. Before her paralegal certification and that bachelor's degree from Oregon, she didn't exist. No social media, no residential history, no school records. That's highly unusual for anyone her age. Especially now, when even people trying to stay off the grid still leave digital footprints."

My heart picked up speed. It was exactly what I'd found when I searched for Heather myself. *Nothing.*

Braden frowned. "So what does that mean? She's using a fake identity?"

Emily's lips tightened. "Not exactly. My investigator is a retired FBI agent who also worked for the DA's office, so he knows the system, and he found a trace. A legal name change, about five years ago. But when he tried to pull the original record, he hit a wall."

"A wall?" I asked.

"The file's sealed," Emily said.

"Why would a name change be protected?" Braden asked.

"That's the $64,000 question right now," Emily said. "We're digging around, but the seal makes it almost impossible to access the record without a warrant." She leaned forward, her voice lowering slightly. "That's a tough nut to crack, but we're working on it."

For a moment, none of us spoke. My pulse was in my throat.

Heather seemed to have a vanished past, and that was something I knew a lot about.

A chill rippled through me. What if her lawyer was digging into mine? Like Emily was digging into Heather's.

Emily glanced from me to Braden, her tone sharpening, snapping me out of my thoughts.

"Whoever Heather Evans used to be, she went to great lengths to bury it. And people who bury their pasts deeply usually have something worth hiding."

Don't I know it, I thought.

"Give my PI a few days. But for now, lay low. Especially you, Braden."

BRADEN and I rode the elevator down in stunned silence. Outside, the air felt crisp and clean, almost forgiving. I wanted to tell him the truth about my past, but I couldn't. Not now. Not when things finally seemed to be turning for him. He looked lighter, almost hopeful.

"I knew there was something off about her. That liar," he said.

I met his eyes and felt the weight of my own lies pressing down. But right now, we needed a common enemy. Heather Evans would do.

"I swear on my life, Jenna, I did not sleep with that woman."

For the first time in days, I believed him.

"Let's go home," I said.

TWENTY-ONE

MORNING LIGHT SPILLED THROUGH THE SHEER curtains, soft and golden, painting the room in warmth I hadn't felt in weeks. Braden's chest rose and fell beneath my cheek, steady, solid, familiar. For the first time in what felt like forever, the air between us wasn't heavy with silence or accusation.

His arm was draped lazily across my hip, his heartbeat steady against my ear. That sound used to comfort me. It still did.

Last night replayed in my mind. The drive home from Emily's office, the tension beginning to melt as we drove across the Golden Gate Bridge, that faint spark of hope flickering back to life between us. On a whim, we'd stopped at the In-N-Out off the 101 near Vista Bay. Lucy's favorite.

After a week at the condo, she'd squealed when

Braden walked through the door, then she'd squealed even louder when she saw him clutching a paper bag that smelled like heaven and grease. "Daddy!" she'd cried, and for a few blissful hours, we were a family again.

We ate on the patio as the sun dipped. Braden and Lucy had strawberry shakes with their burgers; I stuck with chocolate—always did. Sunny sat at our feet, laser-focused on Lucy, knowing she was his best shot at a stray fry. For a while, it almost felt normal again.

We laughed. Talked about school, about Lucy's volcano science project; she'd gotten an A.

We didn't mention lawsuits, viral videos, clickbait headlines, arrests, bail, or restraining orders. Not once. For a few stolen hours, the world shrank back down to something simple: burgers, milkshakes, family.

Later that night, after Lucy went to bed, Braden and I found each other again. No words, just a need to reconnect, to remind ourselves that beneath all the wreckage, there was still an *us*. That night, the intimacy drought ended. There was the close heat of someone you've both loved and lost, all in the same breath.

Now, in the quiet morning light, I should've felt whole. But my mind wouldn't stop.

The lawsuit still loomed like a thundercloud on the horizon, but that wasn't what kept me awake. We could fight that. We had Emily Acosta—one of the best in the city. We had money, lawyers, and strategy.

What I didn't have was peace.

Because I believed him now. I truly did. Braden hadn't slept with Heather Evans. He hadn't harassed her. He hadn't done any of the things she'd accused him of.

But if that was true, then why had Heather done this to him? To our family?

There was the lawsuit, but still no demand for settlement, nor was there a monetary demand on the lawsuit. If she wasn't after money, then what?

Why target him? Why destroy our lives? Go to such lengths? Because he spurned her advances?

I'd turned those questions over in my head all night, searching for logic where there was none. Revenge? Money? Some kind of obsession?

My thoughts kept circling the same dark center that told me Heather's motives were deeper, darker.

That terrified me more than anything.

I closed my eyes and pressed closer to Braden, breathing him in. His hand brushed lightly through my hair, half-asleep, half-instinctual.

"I love you," he murmured.

I froze. Part of me wanted to say it back; the other part was tangled in fear.

Would he still love me if he found out I'd been lying to him since the day we met?

I told myself it wasn't really lying. Just not telling him everything about my past. But lying by omission is still lying. From the day we met, I wanted to be honest with him.

I was twenty-one when I met Braden at a house party in Palo Alto. I was a junior at Cal State East Bay, in Hayward. He was twenty-five, a third-year law student at Stanford.

All the girls at the party swooned when Braden arrived. He stepped through the doorway like he owned the air around him. The low hum of music and laughter seemingly dipped for half a beat as heads turned. He wore faded black jeans that fit like they were made for him, a charcoal Ralph Lauren Henley long-sleeve shirt, the top buttons undone just enough to hint at confidence. The red stitching of the tiny polo logo seemed to come alive as he walked. The silver glint of his watch caught the light when he moved.

Every detail looked unplanned yet perfect. The rolled sleeves, the worn leather belt. He wasn't overdressed but somehow made half the guys in the room look like they were trying too hard, and the other half like slobs.

Conversations faltered; a few girls exchanged glances, pretending not to stare. He smiled, just slightly, and the room seemed to shift toward him.

In a room full of frat boys in baseball caps, he stood out.

I'd never seen such confidence. One of my friends whispered that he was a *Morrissey*, as if that explained everything. I didn't grow up in the land of tech money and old-money trust funds, so I had no clue about the Morrissey family's blue blood bona fides. I'd always been evasive about my upbringing. It felt safer that way, easier to blend in where the median household income was double the national average.

But even I could tell Braden came from privilege.

It was silly, but when he picked *me* to talk to that night, out of all the other girls in that room eager to be picked, I felt giddy and warm, like the lucky contestant whose name had just been called on *The Price Is Right*.

My guard was up, though. Every girl knew the rules of college parties: only drink from bottles you opened yourself. Never take a cup from a stranger.

Braden was a perfect gentleman that first night. We talked for hours. I was impressed to learn he was in his final year of law school—at Stanford, no less. That's why he left early; he had to study. When he asked for my number, I practically blurted it out before he'd finished talking.

He typed it into his phone, sent a quick test text. My phone pinged—proof I hadn't given him a fake number. *"Nice to meet you. 😉 "* the message read. I laughed. Then he was gone.

. . .

WE TEXTED FOR WEEKS, then went out on a few dates. On our second date, he kissed me, and my knees buckled.

He was blue blood; I was blue collar. He drove a new BMW; it was public transportation for me. I felt like our story was straight out of *Pretty in Pink*. But I knew, despite our different worlds, that he was *the one*.

As things grew serious, we started sharing stories about our pasts: families, childhoods, all the getting-to-know-you things. I knew I should tell him the truth about mine.

But I kept putting it off.

Until nineteen years had passed.

And here I was, in bed with my husband, the father of my child, who still didn't know my secret and the terrible thing I had done as a teenager.

TWENTY-TWO

I HAD BEEN WAITING FOR THIS DAY FOR YEARS. THE fewer days left, the slower time seemed to crawl. But it was finally time. I was being released.

A CO we'd nicknamed Porky because he was short and pudgy with a snubbed nose came to get me at my cell, his demeanor indifferent. He could care less if I stayed or went.

For me, this day was monumental. But I played it cool. As if I weren't in a hurry.

"Let's go!" Porky barked, as I was taking my time.

I folded the gray state-issue clothes on my cot one last time—neat, sharp corners, the way I'd learned to do everything here because order was safety in this place. Chaos got you in trouble.

Monalisa stood by the wall, arms crossed, chewing her gum like nothing could touch her. But I knew better. Hurt flickered behind her dark eyes, fast and stubborn—she'd rather die than let Porky see her cry.

We'd already had our real goodbye last night, after lights out, when nobody could see her cry.

"Don't go soft out there, girl," she said. "The outside world's colder than this place."

"I know."

"Yeah? Then don't forget what I taught you in here."

"I won't."

She smirked. "You'll be fine, Meryl. You're smart and mean when you have to be."

"Thanks for having my back all these years," I said.

"Going to miss your ass."

It almost sounded like love.

Porky shouted again, keys jangling, impatient.

"Move it! Or do you want to stay locked up with your girlfriend?" he said with a smirk.

Like he had any say about that.

I looked back one last time. Monalisa stepped closer, gripping the bars. "Don't forget me."

"I won't," I lied.

"Dykes," the guard muttered under his breath. Low enough to deny it later, loud enough for us to hear.

Monalisa's eyes went cold. I knew that look — he'd regret uttering that slur at us. Monalisa would make sure of that.

I laughed.

After I was processed out, another guard walked me towards the front gate. The hallway between the prison side and the outside felt like a tunnel between worlds. Even the smell changed as I walked. Bleach and metal gave way to something like sunlight and exhaust fumes from parking lot.

Once outside, the air felt too big. The sky too wide. The sun was bright and wrong on my face. But it felt good. I blinked at it like a newborn.

The guard handed me a manila envelope stamped with the state seal. Inside were my discharge papers, gate money, my GED certificate, my probation officer's contact info, and a schedule from the community college I'd been enrolled in. As soon as I could, I planned to transfer to a real college.

"Good luck," he said.

And that was it. It was strange. Had I stepped out here an hour ago, they would have shot me. Now the guard walked away leaving me alone. For him, I was someone else's problem now, I suppose.

I had no one waiting for me. No family, no friends, no one to hug me or tell me they missed me. Just the detention center's shuttle bus parked at the curb, engine idling, the driver's eyes glazed with bureaucracy, but at least I had a ride to town so I could stretch out the small release stipend the DOC handed out to freed inmates like myself. It wasn't much, but it should get me away from this place.

I had almost six figures waiting for me in a savings account. Thanks to a settlement with the state for fostering me to a pedo.

It was the most money I ever had in my whole life. But I knew it wouldn't last too long, especially in California; it would give me a few years to get my bearings. Get my education.

I wasn't too worried about the future. I would figure things out. Monalisa always encouraged me to use my brains. "You're a smart motherfucker," she would tell me time and again.

When I was outside, I got my hands on all types of books to help. I would read anything practical. Social engineering manuals, DMV guides, a battered copy of an old legal primer. "Learn how the system thinks," she'd said. "Then think it better."

But all that could wait. Right now I just wanted to savor the fact that for the first time in my life, I was free. I wasn't a ward or an inmate of the state.

Not that it wasn't a scary feeling.

In there, I'd been somebody. I'd had protection, a name. Power. Respect. I'd had Monalisa. Out here, I was a ghost again. Nobody.

But that would change because I was going to make it happen.

The way I saw it, I wasn't starting over. I was starting *fresh*. A new life, and I was going to make the most of it. I wasn't going to end up back there. Or under the thumb of anyone.

I'd learned what mattered: people believed what you showed them, not who you were. And if you played the right part long enough, the world would cast you accordingly.

The thought made me smile.

They said I'd been rehabilitated.

They said I could go out and build something new.

They had no idea what I was going to build.

Monalisa showed me how to get information you can hold over people. The kind that makes them do what you want.

TWENTY-THREE

It had been a few days since we'd heard from Emily Acosta.

And although I welcomed the respite from our problems as we reconnected, again husband and wife, working hard at trying to be a family, Braden's legal troubles still hung over us like a dark cloud about to unleash a tsunami.

Braden had warned me. The legal system moves at a sloth's pace. We'd probably be mired in this world for a year or two, if we were lucky.

So when Emily texted that she'd be calling at 12:30, we were nervous but also hopeful. Maybe this call would finally bring answers. Maybe Heather Evans would finally make sense, and we could figure a way to stop her reign of terror over our family.

The minutes before the call seemed like hours.

Braden kept pacing between the kitchen and the living room window, glancing at his phone every thirty seconds.

I tried to read, but my eyes kept tracking the clock on the oven. 12:26. 12:28.

Every tick of the second hand scraped at my nerves.

Emily had confirmed Heather's legal name change. Did Emily now know her real name? Did she have Heather's history beyond the last few years? Beyond the conjuring of Heather Evans, seemingly out of thin air?

Then again, maybe Emily had found nothing.

"What if she didn't find anything?" I finally asked.

Braden didn't look up. "She'll find something. She always does."

He said it like a prayer more than a fact.

The phone rang right on time.

On the first ring Braden answered, glanced at me, then hit the speaker.

"Emily," he said. "You're on."

As usual, she sounded calm, assured, with the kind of tone that could make juries lean forward.

"I've got an update," she said. "My investigator dug deeper into Heather Evans."

My pulse quickened.

We'd been waiting for this, the thing Emily had called *the $64,000 question* when we'd met in her office three days ago.

"Did he get lucky?" Braden asked with a trace of hope.

"It's not luck," Emily said. "Well, lucky for us he's a retired Fed who's too stubborn to play golf every day, so he freelances for me on the tough cases, like this one. You'd like him, Braden. A lawyer's dream investigator. Old-school, relentless, the kind who files paper notes instead of using Evernote. A dog with a bone. Won't stop till he's gnawed it clean."

Braden gave a humorless chuckle. "That's exactly what we need."

"I figured you'd say that," she said with a hint of satisfaction. I could hear papers rustling on her end. "We got her real name."

"Yes!" Braden said, slapping the countertop.

I straightened, the tension palpable.

"What's her real name?" I asked.

"Ashley Holloway."

The way she said it, I could tell she was expecting it to mean something to us. The name hung in the air like static.

I looked at Braden. He shook his head slowly, his brow furrowed. I had no idea who that was either.

"Ring any bells?" Emily asked after a moment of silence, now sounding a bit more demure and less confident.

"Never heard of her," Braden said.

"Same for me," I added.

Emily exhaled, audibly disappointed. "Damn. I was hoping it would mean something to either of you."

Braden leaned forward. "Okay, but now that you have her real name, you've been able to track her down. Where did she come from? Why is she here? Why did she target me?"

"I'm sorry, but I hit another brick wall, even thicker than before. The reason we couldn't see that Heather had changed her name from Ashley Halloway is because that person had a sealed criminal record. Without a court order, we can't get any more information through the traditional route."

My stomach tightened. Not again.

"Traditional route? What does that mean?" I asked.

"It means my PI isn't done digging. He's working his contacts. But that takes a bit more finesse, and time."

Braden rubbed his temples. "So we're dealing with someone who is damned good at covering their tracks."

Emily's tone sharpened. "I wouldn't go that far. It's the state that sealed her record because she was a kid. But they don't do that for some silly little crime, like stealing dad's car. Whatever crime she committed, it was something serious."

Her words landed hard.

Just what the hell were we up against here?

The call ended with promises of more helpful information on Heather Evans, AKA Ashley Holloway.

"Just give it some time," Emily said.

I feared in the pit of my stomach that time was the one

luxury we did not have with this crazy chameleon after Braden.

Braden poured himself something. For a split second, I thought he was reaching for bourbon again. But no, just water. He drank slowly, eyes far away. "Ashley Holloway," he said, testing the name like it might trigger some memory as to who Heather was and what she wanted with us.

"Who the hell are you?"

TWENTY-FOUR

Ashley Halloway.

The name hit me like a blade. I let out a scream so sharp it scraped my throat raw and left my ears ringing. The sound bounced off the cramped walls of my apartment, too loud, too revealing.

Get a grip, I told myself. Panic is for people without options.

I forced a breath in, then out, steadying the tremor in my hands. Losing control — even for a second — was dangerous. Especially in Hayes Valley, where the neighbors pretended to mind their own business but couldn't resist calling the cops if something sounded off. The last thing I needed was a badge at my door asking questions I wouldn't answer.

I pressed my palms against the counter and closed my eyes. The scream had felt good for half a heartbeat — a release valve popping open — but indulgence is weakness. And I didn't do weakness anymore.

Now that I had calmed down, I looked for my phone. I had thrown it across the room in a fit of rage. It had bounced off the couch and landed with a thud on my plush rug, which was better than bouncing off the hardwood floor. I grabbed my phone. I'd lost my cool when I heard them talk to that lawyer.

I hadn't seen this coming. *Emily Acosta*. THE *Emily Acosta*. She was on TV all the time, whoring herself out to the highest bidder.

Still. When Braden hired her, I wasn't worried. Big-name attorneys love billable hours more than their clients. But I hadn't counted on that PI of hers digging into everything like a rabid bloodhound.

I stalked across the room to the small, tidy workstation I had set up by the window. My monitors were still on, one of them displaying a live audio feed from Braden and Jenna's house. Jenna's perfect house. One of my devices sat hidden inside the living room soundbar. A tiny wireless transmitter that cost less than a decent dinner out but worked like a charm. I had six of them planted throughout the house. I could even listen to them taking a dump; not that I was inclined to do so, but I loved that power.

Scrolling back the audio file with my trackpad, I listened again to the conversation from earlier.

Emily's clipped, powerful voice came through the

speakers like a bullet. "We got her real name… Ashley Holloway."

Hearing that again made me shake. I thought I had put it behind me, forever.

For months I'd stayed one step ahead of them. For months I'd been in control. Now a retired Fed with nothing better to do than dig through my life had found the one thing I'd spent years burying.

Of course the damned state would once again fail miserably at their job. A sealed record shouldn't be unsealed to a retired fed boomer with friends he pays off on the inside. It was not fair. The rich always got away with everything.

Still, I had to settle down. All they had was a name. That was it. If the PI could actually access my criminal records, then I was cooked; but even if he could, I had time. I would need to change my plans. Improvise. I'm good at that.

I turned the volume down, breathing through my teeth. "You think you're so smart, Jenna," I whispered to no one. "You think you can outplay me."

Bugging them had been the easy part. I'd memorized their schedules months ago. I knew the keypad code to the garage, the alarm, everything. Braden thought he was careful, protecting his family and big fancy house. He wasn't. That type of shit might keep out some rando burglar off the street, but not someone like me.

I didn't need to break in with a crowbar. All I needed was a PDF document.

During the Hudson merger deal, when PDF documents were flying left and right, I'd sent it to Braden. It looked legit on the surface, just like any of the other documents, but hidden within was a Trojan horse bundled with a keylogger.

Once Braden opened it, I had complete access. From there, it was easy to jump to all his personal devices, and Jenna's too. It's why they call it a virus; it spreads from one machine to the next.

For months, the keylogger gave me everything I needed. Every keystroke, every login, every password. To every app on their smartphones. I could lock them out of their home and cars if I wanted. I had access to his calendar, his inbox, his private documents. He thought everything was locked away behind randomly generated passwords, but I had access to that software as well. It was too easy, and fun.

Braden might have been some hotshot lawyer, but with me he was a sitting duck. And I had plucked him clean.

I opened my screen to their home security app. I logged in and fired up the home-camera feeds. I was looking inside their home in real time.

Their taste in home décor was expensive. They were preparing for dinner. The perfect little family, acting like nothing had happened.

My plan to break them up for good had failed when she'd taken him back, and I'd heard them having sex last night. Her stupid little moans, his caveman-like grunting. So disgusting. But it was proof I was failing.

Jenna. *God, Jenna.*

Perfect hair. Perfect house. Perfect mother to that spoiled little brat of hers. She was so smug in her suburban bubble, like she'd earned any of it.

I pressed my palms against the cold glass of my window and stared at the street below. Hayes Valley land of the overpriced mimosa was a neighborhood where finding a meal for under thirty dollars and cocktails under fifteen dollars would be a challenge, yet it was packed with people. Everyone down there was living their perfect little lives, not knowing what it took to make yourself since the good stuff was handed to them on a silver platter. I had to claw my way out of hell to get here.

And Braden. His whole perfect life mapped out at conception. Private elite schools starting at kindergarten. And his kind then have the balls to brag about how hard they worked for their success, like it wasn't predestined by being born a fucking millionaire.

Jenna had got there on her back. Marrying that rich asshole. I'd had it all figured out. They weren't supposed to win. *I* was.

But as much as I hated to admit it, Jenna had proven me wrong. I thought she was just this vapid suburban rich mom who would do nothing, but when she began doing research on her computer about me, I could see she had skills I didn't know she had.

It was time to hit them harder. I'd been patient. So patient. The paralegal certificate. The job interview. Getting myself ensconced in his law firm. In his team.

I loved seeing him unravel. Death by one thousand paper cuts. The lawsuit. The humiliation. The whispers. Watching their perfect world splinter piece by piece.

But patience only gets you so far.

I walked back to my desk and opened the encrypted files on my hard drive. A digital graveyard of everything I'd collected. Passwords, financial records, browser histories. Every inch of Braden's life, mapped out and color-coded. I could ruin him five different ways by sundown. But that wasn't the plan. I wanted him to *feel* it. I wanted her to *feel* it.

The HR complaint and lawsuit had been the opening act. The leaks to *TTU* and the media circus they triggered was delicious, as was getting him arrested. He was so easy to push into whatever I wanted him pushed.

But now, because of Emily Acosta, I had to pivot.

On the screen, Lucy bounced into the kitchen, Mom and Dad doting on her, like always. Such a spoiled little brat. Just like her father, with a privileged life laid out in front of her.

A slow, deliberate smile crept across my face.

Braden loved that little girl. Jenna had built her entire world around her. Lucy was the shining, untouchable centerpiece of their little fairytale.

And every fairytale has a monster.

TWENTY-FIVE

THE TEXT CAME JUST AS I WAS TURNING INTO THE school parking lot.

UNKNOWN: You think you can waltz back to your perfect life? Think again. The path ahead makes what you've faced so far seem like a gentle stroll.

It had been days since I'd gotten one of these ominous, threatening text messages. It took a moment for it to sink in as I stared at the screen, the steering wheel slick beneath my palms. This had to be Heather. Or Ashley. Or whatever that psycho's real name was. And for sure she was the caller using that creepy voice distorter who late at night just said *goodnight.*

What the hell did she want with our family?

My pulse thudded in my ears like a drum. But this text felt different. The earlier texts had been vague, the kind of thing you could almost wave off as trolling or harassment after Braden became good fodder for the social media mob and gossip columnists. We had creeps crawling out of basements to send us nasty messages. But this one had teeth. Cold, sharpened teeth. It wasn't a taunt. It was a promise.

A chill slid down my spine. I thought about calling 911, but what could they do about an anonymous text?

Emily. My hands were shaking as I pressed the side button and forwarded the text to Emily's number. The tires crackled over the asphalt as I eased into a parking spot.

I killed the engine but didn't move. Outside, the schoolyard looked deceptively normal. Kids swung their backpacks, parents chatted with water bottles in hand, cars lined up in neat little rows like nothing bad ever happened here. A bubble of safety or the illusion of it.

As I couldn't stay in the car all rattled by that message, I finally shoved the door open and climbed out. The gentle breeze felt nice. My eyes scanned the sea of small faces coming out of the gates, searching for Lucy's hair—chestnut with that stubborn curl at the ends she hated. My girl. My heartbeat. My reason.

She'd made me promise pancakes for dinner this morning, her hair still wild from sleep, pink sweatshirt half-zipped as she told me a long, rambling story about a science experiment that "wasn't supposed to explode but did." Braden had leaned against the kitchen island, coffee in hand, watching her with that soft look he saved just for her.

Like she was the only good thing left in the world. He'd winked at me over her head, and for a rare moment, it felt like we were all okay. Like things were going to get better. Like before.

Except... I didn't see her.

"Jenna?"

I turned at the sound of my name. Mrs. Keller, one of Lucy's teachers, walked toward me, squinting in confusion. "Did Lucy forget something?"

The question didn't make sense. "What? No. I just got here. I'm here to pick her up."

Mrs. Keller blinked, her brow furrowing. "I thought you already picked her up."

For half a second, the world went silent. A thin, whistling kind of silence that doesn't belong to daylight.

"No. I just got here," I repeated, looking past her, expecting to see Lucy bouncing down the steps with a *Hiya, Mom.*

Mrs. Keller's face shifted; confusion melted into unease. "I'm sure she was picked up. I saw her leaving earlier. In your car," she said, pointing toward my black Cayenne.

Panic started as a prickling at the back of my neck, then spread fast, flooding my chest. "No. I just got here," I repeated once again, each time more sharply. "Where is my daughter?"

Mrs. Keller turned, calling to a couple of other teachers. "Lucy Morrissey," she said. "Did anyone see Lucy leave?"

Another teacher, Mr. Owens, stepped closer. "She's already gone. Her mom picked her up. Black Porsche Cayenne. I'm sure it was you," he said, looking at me. But I could see the doubt flicker in his eyes as he looked more closely.

My stomach turned to ice. "No. No, it wasn't me. Are you saying she got into someone else's car?" I felt dizzy.

They paled in unison, then exchanged furtive glances as if one of them might have a simple answer as to where Lucy was.

All they could mutter were half attempts to reassure me.

My panic exploded. I felt my knees wobble, but some primal part of me warned: *Don't lock your knees, you'll pass out.*

"Lucy!" I shouted, spinning, scanning the throng of people. Parents turned to look. Some instinctively drew their children closer.

The casual after-school chatter dimmed as if someone had turned down the volume.

Teachers began to fan out. A few froze. Others moved, voices raised, calling Lucy's name. Aside from an active shooter, this was their worst nightmare. Mr. Owens was shouting hoarsely for the school resource officer.

I clutched my phone, hands trembling so hard I nearly dropped it. The last text echoed in my head like a curse.

The path ahead makes what you've faced so far seem like a gentle stroll.

I stabbed at the screen and hit 911.

"My daughter's missing," I said as soon as the dispatcher answered. My voice cracked on the word *daughter*.

By the time they patched me through, a small crowd had gathered at the gate. Teachers moved in sharp, anxious lines. Parents whispered. So many faces blurred into a collage of pity and fear.

"She's eleven," I told the dispatcher. "Brown hair. Pink sweatshirt with a unicorn patch on the left sleeve. She was supposed to be here. I just got here. The teachers told me someone took her."

The dispatcher's calm, practiced tone tried to tether me down. "Ma'am, I need you to stay on the line. Officers are on the way. Do you know the exact time she was last seen?"

"No!" The sound from me was sharp and ugly. "They thought it was me!"

"Breathe for me, ma'am. You're doing great."

No, I wasn't. I was hanging by a frayed thread.

I spun in circles, scanning the street for every black SUV. Every flash of metal, every car backing out of the lot suddenly felt like the enemy.

I ran to the gate. I yelled her name. "Lucy!"

Nothing.

A siren wailed faintly in the distance. My legs shook so hard I had to grab the chain-link fence to stay upright.

"She was picked up early," Mrs. Keller kept saying, as if she repeated it enough, time would rewind and everything would be fine.

"By whom?" I snapped, turning on her. My voice came out raw, unrecognizable. "Who signed her out?"

Mrs. Keller faltered, pale. "The front office should... I'll check."

She bolted inside, probably grasping at the excuse to go hide in the school

Someone touched my shoulder, a father from Lucy's class. His face was tight with pity. "Hey, they'll find her. Okay? Kids don't just vanish."

I jerked away. Yes, they do. And he didn't understand. Lucy wasn't "kids." Lucy was *my* kid. Easy for him to say that when he was holding his kid's hand. He meant well, but I wanted to deck him as I broke free and ran towards my car. None of these people could help me.

This wasn't random. This was the storm the text had promised. It was Heather. I knew it.

The siren grew louder. The resource officer came running out of the school. People were whispering now. I could hear my name, snippets: *Jenna Morrissey, the video, her husband, that scandal.*

The flash of a vehicle caught my eye: a Porsche Cayenne turning onto the main road a block away. My heart leapt. But it was the wrong color, red, not black like mine. My chest tightened.

My phone buzzed again.

UNKNOWN: *Run all you want. I'm already ahead of you.*

A few seconds later, another text.

UNKNOWN: *Lucy says hi.*

The world tilted.

"Love you, Mommy."

Her little voice echoed in my head—bright, careless, full of trust. It sliced through me like glass that I wasn't there for her. That I let this happen to her.

Lucy's giggle floated up in my memory—high and quick, the way she laughed when I tickled her under the chin and pretended to "steal" her nose when she was younger. "I'll race you, Mom!" she'd shrieked last weekend, running barefoot on the beach.

I clutched the phone so hard my hand was cramping.

For a second, I couldn't see straight. I thought I was going to pass out.

Behind me, Mrs. Keller's words tumbled out to the officer: Lucy had been picked up thirty minutes ago. Mr. Owens added, "She looked just like Mrs. Morrissey."

I couldn't stand still. I turned and bolted toward my car. The resource officer yelled my name, but I didn't acknowledge him. What good was he now? Where had he been when Heather kidnapped her? Lucy was gone.

Next thing I knew, I was in my car, peeling out of the parking lot, my heart pounding so hard it blurred the edges of everything else.

Lucy was out there.

And Heather had her.

I texted back to the unknown number that sent me those texts.

If you hurt my daughter, I am going to kill you.

TWENTY-SIX

I FLOORED IT.

The Cayenne surged, its supercharged twin-turbo V8 engine crackling as I winded down a road from the school to the main thoroughfare, towards the 101 ramp.

It's what I would do, if I were her. Head towards the freeway. The open road.

I blew through a red light, cars honked, a man flipped me off. I kept going. That was all I could do.

Lucy was out there somewhere.

My hands were slick on the wheel, my heart slamming against my chest. I needed to do something. Anything.

Then it hit me. Lucy's phone.

She wasn't allowed to turn off location tracking. That had been our deal. If she disabled it, she lost phone privileges.

I fumbled for mine, nearly dropping it as I opened *Find My Phone*. The loading wheel spun, my breath catching on every spin, then there it was.

A blue dot.

She was close. Less than two miles away. Near the 101 ramp.

And the dot wasn't moving.

"Oh God," I whispered, flooring it.

Maybe Heather had realized she'd gone way too far, pulled over and let Lucy out of the car. I desperately wanted to believe that as my eyes scanned the shoulder of the road.

Tires screamed as I swerved onto the shoulder near the location that the GPS indicated for the phone. I jumped out, gravel biting into my sneakers. The wind from passing cars whipped at my hair as I scanned the embankment.

Then I saw it.

Lucy's pink phone lay face down in the dirt. The Swifty stickers she'd plastered on the back were peeling at the edges.

She would never leave that phone behind. Not voluntarily.

I crouched to get it and almost passed out, but I recovered and scooped it up. It was still warm.

My phone rang. Braden's name lit up on the dash.

I sprinted back to the car, slammed the door, and answered.

"Jenna, oh God, did you find her?"

I shook my head, though he couldn't see me. "No. Just her phone. I found it by the highway ramp."

"Jenna, listen to me," he said, trying to sound steady. "The police are on their way here. They're coordinating units. An Amber Alert will be going out soon. You need to come home. Let them handle this."

"No," I snapped. "I can't just *sit* there while she's out here. I can't."

"Jenna, you're in no condition to drive; if you crash the car looking for her, you'll only make things worse. For Lucy. For us."

I pressed my forehead against the steering wheel, breath shaky. "I can't just—"

"We're going to find her," he said firmly. "We *will*. Just come home. Please."

The highway didn't care. The cars kept screaming past like nothing had happened.

"Braden, she has our little girl," I whispered.

"You know who took her?"

"Heather. Who else?"

A beat of silence. "Jesus Christ," he mumbled as if he hadn't thought she was behind this as well.

I hung up before he could say anything else. Because I couldn't listen to logic. Logic wasn't going to bring my daughter back.

I gripped the wheel and I peeled back into traffic. I had

two choices. North or South. I turned the wheel and merged onto 101 North on pure instinct.

NORTHBOUND TRAFFIC CRAWLED at this time, a slow river of metal and red brake lights lined up ahead of me seemingly for miles. I gripped the wheel so hard my hands ached, my eyes flicking from car to car.

Black sedan. Black SUV. Another crossover with tinted windows. Every one of them could've been the car. But none of them were.

The teacher said the kidnapper was in a black Porsche Cayenne like my car. That couldn't be a coincidence. How long had she planned to do this? Even after the hell she had put us through, I never thought she would do something like this. Who kidnaps a child. And why? I'm sure there was a reason she wanted to hurt Braden. Me, even. But an innocent child?

My chest burned from trying to see through layers of glass and steel, willing a flash of Lucy's chestnut hair to appear behind one of those windshields.

Nothing.

The green highway sign overhead blurred past—*San Rafael 6 miles*—but I barely saw it. All that mattered was the seemingly endless line of black cars on the highway. I didn't realize how many were out on the road. Too many. Everywhere.

I leaned forward over the wheel as if that would sharpen my vision, as if I could force the world to give me what I needed. A horn blared behind me when I cut too close into the next lane. One of those long, angry ones. That person wouldn't be driving so well if their child had been kidnapped.

Lucy was out there somewhere. Maybe in one of these cars. Maybe not in any of them. Where was she?

My throat closed, and for a moment the highway blurred into streaks of color and noise. The steady thrum of tires on the road turned cruel, like a heartbeat I couldn't control.

My pulse pounded. My breathing grew shallow.

I kept looking.

Another black SUV.

Another set of tinted windows.

Another reflection of my own terrified face staring back at me.

Hopelessness hit hard and low, a weight on my chest I couldn't shake. I could drive like this all day; scanning, searching, praying, and it might not matter.

I pressed harder on the gas. Another horn. Someone flipped me off again when I cut them off.

"Come on," I urged. "Come on, Lucy. Give me something."

But the highway didn't answer. Just the howl of wind

against metal and the red taillights of strangers who could not know my world had just split in two.

I was about to pull over, the weight of everything pressing down like a hand on my chest, when my phone rang.

Emily Acosta.

I fumbled for the screen like it was a lifeline.

Her voice came through the car's speaker, calm and steady, the exact opposite of the chaos ripping through me.

"Jenna, I was finalizing my report when your texts came in. Braden filled me in about Lucy. I'm so sorry. I never imagined she'd escalate like this."

The words *she'd escalate like this* twisted in my chest.

At least Emily saw it too: Heather had taken Lucy.

Now I just needed answers.

"My PI managed to dig up more on Heather Evans," Emily said. "Or rather, Ashley Holloway. He was finally able to get the lowdown on that sealed record. Don't ask how."

I gripped the wheel. I could care less how he'd got the information.

"She was fifteen when she killed her foster father. Shot him with a 12-gauge shotgun." Emily said. "He'd been abusing her for months, so she got a sweet deal due to her age, and because of the abuse. So at eighteen they cut her loose and sealed her minor record. Clean slate."

She sounded clinical, detached, like she was reading a deposition.

But the words sank like stones.

Fifteen. Foster care. Murder.

How does that turn into *this*? Kidnapping my Lucy? And three years for murder? How did she pull that off, even with the abuse?

Emily continued.

"The system that failed her tried to protect her," Emily said. "When she changed her name, she basically erased Ashley Holloway from existence."

I didn't think I could feel more fear than I had this past hour, but knowing Lucy was in the hands of a convicted killer did just that. Whatever horrors she'd endured, she'd still pulled a trigger and killed a human being. And now she had my daughter.

None of this made sense. Why Braden? It was not as if he had anything to do with Heather ending up in foster care. What happened to her? Why wasn't she adopted?

That word—*adoption*—always sent shivers down my spine and tied my stomach in knots.

Adoption.

I slammed on the brakes and veered onto the shoulder. Horns exploded behind me. The car jolted to a stop, and I sat there shaking, the steering wheel slick under my hands.

"Jenna?" Emily's voice crackled through the speaker. "Are you there?"

I swallowed hard. "Do you...do you have Heather's date of birth?"

A pause. Paper rustling.

"Uh, yeah, hold on." A moment later, she was back, "January 17, 2002. Why?"

The air went thin. I felt it leave my body.

"That can't be right," I whispered.

"It's right," she said gently. "Why? Does the date mean something to you?"

My throat burned with bile. I couldn't answer at first.

Because saying it would make it real.

I pressed a trembling hand to my mouth. The memory came like a flood. The smell of disinfectant, a nurse turning away, my mother wouldn't look at me. My father refused to be there. I was sixteen years old, the sheet pulled up to my chin as I sobbed uncontrollably. The sound of a baby crying, its cry fading as they carried the newborn baby out of my room. *My baby.*

"Jenna?" Emily said again, sounding more worried now. "Talk to me."

The words scraped out of me, quiet, broken.

"I got pregnant when I was sixteen," I said.

I couldn't remember the last time I'd said that to anyone. The last time I'd said it out loud.

"My parents forced me to give her up. I never even held her. My daughter. My first-born daughter was born on January 17, 2002."

The car was silent except for my ragged breathing and the rush of traffic outside.

Emily didn't speak. There was nothing to say.

Heather Evans.

Ashley Holloway.

My daughter.

TWENTY-SEVEN

Driving away with Lucy from the school was much easier than I'd imagined. Too easy, really. That's the thing about preparation: It makes you bold.

I rented the black Porsche Cayenne on Turo. I made sure it was the same model and color as Jenna's car. I couldn't find one from the same year as hers, but this was just a year older, so I was certain that wouldn't be a problem. No one looks closely enough anyway at that type of stuff.

In the mirror, I studied my hair, tucked in a low ponytail, my soft makeup, the high, smoky cheekbones Jenna sculpted with a million little products I'd watched her use for months now. I'd practiced her smile until I could do it in my sleep. I'd been watching her for over a year. You learn what people wear, how they purse their lips, where they tuck their hair. Mannerisms are easy to pick up if you pay attention.

I knew how to pass for her.

I wore her perfume, the one she liked to spritz in the morning. I'd watched enough of her on video to know the cadence of her voice when she talked on the phone. At brunch with her vapid idiot friend. I had watched her drop off and pick up Lucy so many times that I knew what to do. All confidence, no hesitation. I belonged there.

With my own phone to my ear as I pulled into the car line, I pretended to argue with a nonexistent assistant about documents, keeping my head down, keeping my eyes on the schoolyard.

The teacher bent down and smiled at me, gave me an idiotic wave.

At first, Lucy wasn't paying close attention either as she climbed into the car and buckled in, assuming I was Jenna. But that only lasted for a few seconds, until she looked at me and hesitated. Kids are smarter than adults give them credit for. I knew that firsthand.

She looked at me the way animals look at strange people in their home: curious, wary. But I was already driving away. Child-safety lock engaged.

"You're not my mom," she said the second she was buckled in, small, stunned, the truth like a pebble tossed across a pond.

I gave a big and syrupy smile. "I know, silly." I sounded like Jenna. I showed her my work badge, the firm's plastic logo flashing with authority. "I'm Heather. I worked for your dad."

That sounded better than, "I worked with your dad before I got his ass fired." It made me smile for real.

She looked at me with uncertainty. She wasn't buying it. Of course she wasn't. I made my voice softer. "Your mom and dad had to go into the city for a last-minute meeting. Your dad asked me to pick you up and bring you home."

"I didn't get a text from my mom about that," she said, looking at me and around the car with suspicion.

I shrugged. "Just doing your dad a favor," I said, trying the practiced placation. "What grade are you in?" I asked, trying to change the subject.

"Fifth," she said, turning away, trying to pretend to look for something in her backpack. She was small and lithe, moving fast like children do, acting practical but clunky.

She pulled out her phone and hunched over it, trying to shield it from me; insulting that she thought I wouldn't notice.

I lunged, fast as in the prison fights, and the phone was in my hand.

"Hey!" she said. I didn't plan to throw it out the window, but I did—and it felt almost cathartic, watching her lose the world between her small fingers as her phone vanished into a ditch.

She screamed. The sound ricocheting between the doors made my ears ring. She tried the door. Locked.

She was getting louder. Shrieking. Annoying.

I slapped the steering wheel, sharply enough for her to stop her antics and look at me with utter fear. Good.

Then I arranged my bag so the gun was visible. A polished Ruger with a matte finish and the scent of oil still on it. I didn't brandish it. I didn't have to. The line of sight is a promise; you don't need to follow through for them to understand.

She froze, looking at it. The fight left her as if someone had pulled a plug. I let the wheel turn and watched the open road unspool ahead.

"Listen, Lucy," I said, very softly. "I'm sorry. I lost my temper. I just wanted to get to know you. Just for a while. I'll take you back to your parents before you know it." That was a lie.

Lucy sniffed. Tears pooled at the corners of her eyes like dew. "I want to go home now."

I watched her the way people watch a movie with a bad ending they can't look away from. Her small fists twisted in the fabric of her hoodie. The resemblance to Jenna was only faint, but there: the slope of the nose, the angle of the jaw. She smelled faintly of strawberry lip balm.

"Your mom never told you about me?" I asked, knowing the answer.

Lucy looked at me, tears trickled down her cheeks. She shook her head.

"I'm your sister," I said.

Now she looked at me as if I had told her I was an alien from another planet.

Again she shook her head, tears flicking from her face like water from a dog drying itself off. One of them landed on my forearm.

"I don't have a sister," she finally said.

"You do," I said. "I'm your older sister."

She didn't believe me. Why would she? Her wonderful, perfect, all-loving mother had never told her about me. It was as if I'd never existed to her.

"Well, we're half-sisters," I added. "Do you know what that means?"

Lucy nodded.

"That's right, same mom, different dads," I said.

The road blurred by. The highway sign said, *San Rafael, six miles*. The GPS fed me nothing but metal and the faintly wailing engines of a life I was still stealing. I watched a cop car pull off at an exit and felt no ripple of fear. Fear is for people who have something left to lose. I had planned for that, too.

We were close to the park-and-ride. I needed to ditch this car.

"That's not true," she said. "Mommy would have told me if I had a sister."

I scoffed. *She doesn't know the real Jenna.*

"Some families hide things," I said. "Some people are protected by the past."

She looked at me, searching for the story that made sense.

I exited the highway and pulled into the Caltrans Park & Ride in Novato, and I parked.

Lucy unleashed a barrage of questions, one after another. "Where are we?" "What are you doing?" "I want my mom."

I looked around; the lot was empty. I reached into my handbag and saw her freeze in fear. She probably thought I was reaching for my gun. I pulled out a syringe.

"What are you doing? Please, no!"

She was so tiny she didn't have a chance as pinned her against the passenger door, and stuck the needle right into her neck artery, as I had practiced many times before. It didn't take long. Not as fast as in the movies, but the propofol did its thing as my little sister went limp.

TWENTY-EIGHT

I PUSHED THE CAYENNE NORTH AT NINETY MILES AN hour, swerving through traffic like someone who'd left reason miles behind. And I had. My palms were slick on the steering wheel. Butterflies whipped through my stomach. I'd never driven this recklessly in my life.

Emily's voice crackled through the car's speakers. It kept me from falling into the abyss. She could hear me driving like a madwoman.

"You can't drive like that," she snapped, sharp and controlled. "You're going to wreck out. Pull over. Let me send a deputy to your location."

Not sure why, but I let out a thin, humorless laugh. She was right. My vision had that haloed shimmer you get when you stand up too fast or cry too long. My breathing came shallow and fast. Dizziness tightened around the edges of my vision. If I crashed out here, Lucy wouldn't have anyone to save her.

"I'm pulling over," I said.

The tires hissed against the shoulder. As the car stopped, a strange calm slid over me.

"Does Braden know?" Emily asked more steadily.

I'd spent two decades building a wall around this secret. And in a single breath, it had cracked.

"No," I whispered. "I never told him. I've never told anyone."

"Oh, Jenna." She didn't say it like a rebuke. She said it like a woman reading the weight I'd carried for twenty-three years. "That's huge. You don't have to carry it alone."

I tried to tell myself that the matching birth dates meant nothing. Coincidence. But I knew better. My mind was just trying to keep me from shattering.

"You have to let the police handle this," Emily said, the lawyer in her surfacing. "They can lock down routes, push alerts, and coordinate units. You driving around like a chicken with its head cut off will only complicate things."

I agreed with what she was telling me. I knew that is what I should be doing. But the image of Lucy, small and terrified as she stood next to Heather, was a knife twisting in my gut. I couldn't sit on the sidelines. Not now.

"Emily, I appreciate that," I said shakily. "But I can't sit still."

"Do you even know where you're going?"

"No."

"At the very least, go home, Jenna. Braden is there with the police. I'm on my way over there. I'm crossing the bridge right now and will be at your place soon to guide you both through this," Emily pleaded.

"I can't do that."

A sigh. "You're a mother in panic. I get it. If it were my kid..." She trailed off. She was a mother. She understood.

"Just promise me you'll slow down."

"I will. Thank you," I said, ending the call.

She was right. I couldn't drive recklessly. I would be of no help to Lucy if I wrecked out and died. And the last thing I wanted now was attention from the cops. Barreling down 101 at ninety miles per hour is something the Highway Patrol tends to notice.

My hands shook as I opened the settings on my phone and killed the tracking apps. I knew it wouldn't make me invisible; the police could still track me via my phone with a warrant, but it would buy me time.

The Cayenne eased back into traffic, this time in a deliberate, measured way. Not because I'd suddenly decided to be rational, but because crashing wasn't an option.

I let the highway swallow me. I passed billboards about mattress sales, and lawyers hocking their personal injury services. I looked at businesses off the highway, but Heather wouldn't go there. Whatever she had planned, it was with purpose. She was heading somewhere.

My mind darted through possibilities the way a terrier races across a field. It seemed that everywhere I looked, I saw Lucy and Heather. But it wasn't them. It was all false sightings.

What had happened to Heather to lead to something like this? Setting up Braden. The TRO and lawsuit. Kidnapping a child—her own half-sister. The realization that this was never about her and Braden, it was between her and me—mother and daughter—hit me like a ton of bricks.

Everything I had put Braden through, kicking him out of the house, accusing him of terrible things, when it was all on me. I was the one with the dark secret. I was the one lying to him, keeping this enormous secret for the eighteen years we'd been together.

Even If I was able to rescue Lucy, could our marriage survive this new avalanche of shit, just as we had emerged from the last heap of misery Heather had unleashed on us?

My phone vibrated. I was planning to ignore all incoming calls and text messages, but I couldn't bear shutting it off just in case Lucy managed to call me. I looked at the caller: Braden.

I answered, "I'm so sorry," before he could speak. "I should have told you."

"Yes. You should have." He sounded flat, as if emotion

cost him too much now. "But I don't have the mental capacity to deal with your lies right now. Not with Lucy missing."

I swallowed the guilt. He was right. Our marriage could wait. Lucy couldn't.

"Of course."

"Come back to the house. The police want to talk to you."

"I can't."

"You mean you won't."

"I have to find her."

A long breath out. "You're not going to run into them by dumb luck, Jenna. She ditched the Cayenne."

"What?"

"They found it abandoned at a CalTrans park-and-ride in Novato. No sign of them."

"Surveillance footage?" I asked.

"No cameras. Probably why she picked it. Cops think she stashed another car there. The rental's a dead end; fake name, fake ID, fake credit card."

The hope in my chest cracked. "I see."

"What the hell are you going to do now?" Braden asked.

"I'm going to find our daughter," I said.

"How?"

"If she switched cars in Novato, she's still heading north. I can feel it."

"Jenna, that's insane. North where? Oregon? Canada?"

"I'll let you know when I get there."

"Come on, Jenna. Lucy needs you here. You're not a cop."

"I'll call you later." My throat ached. "I'm sorry I lied. I know you hate me."

Silence, then the faint sound of his breathing.

"I don't hate you, Jenna," he said finally.

It wasn't forgiveness. But it was something.

I clung to that thought as I steered north toward Lake Tahoe, but the past kept clawing its way to the surface whether I wanted it to or not.

TWENTY-NINE

ALL FOUR TESTS WERE POSITIVE. SIXTEEN AND pregnant wasn't just a reality show on TV now. It was my reality.

I wasn't the first sixteen-year-old to stare at two pink lines as if it were a death sentence. I daydreamed about running away to San Francisco, where rich do-gooders would save me and my baby, but even my fantasies knew better. A girl from our school ran away to LA once—by spring, she was a cautionary tale spreading through school; she was strung out on meth and selling herself on Sunset while parents whispered her name like it was the boogeyman's.

As scared as I was to tell my parents, especially my father, I had no choice. Maybe he'd surprise me, forgive me, take us both in. Help me raise my baby. But that was a fantasy too.

My father was a preacher, a pastor of a small church on the outskirts of Preston, Idaho. It didn't pay much, so he took a day job as the high school guidance counselor. "Both jobs save souls in different ways," he liked to brag.

Our two-bedroom, one-bath house sat tucked behind the church, its white paint peeling from too many cold winters and hot summers. The parsonage always smelled like musk and damp air.

I'd been sitting on the porch swing, staring at the chipped railing, when his voice came through the screen door. Calm. Too calm.

"Jeana," he said. "Come inside."

The way he said my name made my skin go tight. The same cadence he used when he preached. And when he punished.

Jeana. Not Jenna, like I preferred. He was the only one that still used my full, given name which meant *God is gracious*. If only my father was more like that.

The tiny, cluttered living room was stiff with silence. My mother sat at the far end of a well-worn couch that sagged in the middle like a hammock that had seen one too many summers. The frayed arms bowed outward. Her hands were folded in her lap, knuckles bone-white, like those of a woman praying for a miracle that wouldn't come. She didn't look up when I walked in.

My father stood beside the dusty built-in oak bookcase lined with Bibles, Christian themed books—fiction and non-fiction—Sunday bulletins, and family photographs. One of them showed us smiling in front of the church. My smile had always felt borrowed. The photographer yelled, "Smile," so I did.

He motioned for me to sit in the sun-bleached armchair across from him. I obeyed. My heart thudded against my ribs like it was trying to find a way out.

"You have disgraced me, your mother, the church, and worst of all, God," he said, pointing to the ceiling. His brown eyes burned into me. "And for what? A moment of carnal knowledge with that no-good Hansen boy."

He spoke in that Sunday tone—clipped, tinged with judgment; the same he used when talking about sin, damnation, and salvation to his small congregation. He wasn't done preaching.

"Here in my church, I'm looked upon to show my parishioners the way to righteous living. And at school, I'm the one they trust to guide their children toward bright futures. And now, what will they say about you? What will they say about me? I can't even provide proper guidance to my own flesh and blood." His voice rose on the last three words. The way he spat them made me flinch.

I swallowed hard, looking down at the frayed rug. "Sorry—"

He raised his hand, stopping me from speaking. I froze. "Your sorry won't restore my reputation. You have brought shame to this house, to my church. You are a disgrace. If these were ancient times, you'd be stoned to death, as you should be."

Tears blurred my vision. My mother had her eyes squeezed shut, mouthing prayers under her breath, as if she could pray herself to be somewhere else.

The clock on the mantel clicked louder than I remembered. Outside, the porch swing groaned in the wind.

I'd thought again about running away. I'd even looked at ways to end the pregnancy. But I was sixteen, broke, trapped. I told myself maybe he'd soften, maybe he'd forgive me. But that wasn't in his nature. He didn't care about me, or his unborn grandchild. Only about the embarrassment I'd brought to his doorstep.

He paced once. Twice. Then turned back to me, jaw clenched so tight I could see the muscle twitch. I flinched again, expecting another blow like the one I'd gotten earlier when I'd told him I was pregnant.

He didn't hit me this time, but his words hit harder.

"We will fix this. We will make sure your sin does not destroy what I've built here. No one can know about it," he said.

"This is my baby," I whispered.

"No. It's a bastard. A godless abomination." He pointed at my stomach as if it were a curse. "I will not let your shame destroy me."

It was always about him.

My mother flinched but said nothing.

He laid out what was going to happen like a commandment etched in stone.

I would go on a *mission trip* with my mother 120 miles away, to Salt Lake City, Utah. I would live in a home for teenage girls *like me* until the baby was born. Then it would be given to a Christian family. Good, decent people who would love it the way I could not.

I wanted to scream. To tell them I could love my baby. That I would. That I could be a good mother. But my throat closed around the words. Sixteen. No money. No car. No way out. I said nothing.

My mother finally lifted her eyes to me. They were wet and empty.

"Jenna," she whispered. "Please. Don't fight this. It's what's best for all of us. Including the unborn child."

Something in me folded in half that night. I didn't cry. Not then. That came later, when I gave birth to a beautiful, healthy baby girl. When they gently but firmly removed her from my arms and carried her away.

Numb, I stared at the spot where she'd been. It didn't seem real. It was like watching a piece of myself walk out the door with strangers.

They took my baby. I never even got to give her a name.

THIRTY

THINKING ABOUT THE DAY I GAVE UP MY DAUGHTER all those years ago made my eyes sting, like it always did. Keeping it to myself felt like corrosive acid eating through me.

I supposed Heather was doing all this because she'd found me, and she hated me. But despite what she believed, I'd never forgotten her. I thought about her all the time. I couldn't even count the amount of times I thought I'd seen her in a crowd even though I only saw her for a moment as a newborn.

Whenever I read about a successful young woman—an Olympian, a movie star—who even vaguely looked like me, I'd wonder, *could that be my daughter?*

It was a comforting fantasy. In truth, I didn't know what had become of her. I didn't even know if she had stayed and grown up in Utah, where she was born, or if her adopted parents had moved to some other state. I'd tried to find her, but it was a closed adoption; every door I pushed turned into a wall, and every wall put another crack in my heart. So I'd stopped. I'd made myself let go of her, reassured she'd been placed in a loving home.

It was what they had told me on that awful day they took her from me.

When Lucy was born, joy came braided with grief. I felt everything a new mother is supposed to feel, and something else I couldn't name. My firstborn hadn't died, but that's how it had seemed the day they carried her out of my arms. Holding Lucy, I was both ecstatic and hollow, the past rushing in like a riptide.

Braden looked at me with love and concern and, I think, he wrote off my emotional whiplash as normal postpartum blues. I let him think that, since I hadn't told him. I wanted to tell him about my first child, but the spirit of my father still lived in me, though he had died long ago. His warning was louder than my voice: *Tell no one.* How could I have been so scared of a dead man?

That's what he'd told me, over and over, when I came back to Preston. He'd been clear: *Tell no one. And never mention that bastard child again in front of me.* So I did as I was told.

I wiped my eyes, put both hands on the wheel, and turned north for Tahoe.

. . .

THE HIGHWAY LIFTED me toward the mountains like a conveyor belt I couldn't step off. I kept the nose of the car pointed north and tried not to watch the clock. If I stared at minutes, I'd drown in them.

Emily's and Braden's words still hung in my ears—*Slow down, leave it to the cops, be smart*—but my body had switched to some other setting other than reason. I'd let one daughter be taken from me once. I wasn't going to let it happen again.

The green signs ticked past: FAIRFIELD. VACAVILLE. AUBURN. The names blurred into a single command: Keep going up the Sierra Mountains towards Lake Tahoe. I didn't know why; I just felt that was where she was headed.

I kept the speed legal enough not to invite the highway patrol to pull me over. How would I even explain any of this? I could hardly believe it was true.

The ridge line in the distance grew a deeper blue. The air became crisper and thinner up here. The smell of pine wafted into the car through the vents. The usual excitement I had when going up to our mountain cabin, to our city getaway, gave way to a sense of fear and dread this time. I rolled my shoulders and told myself to breathe.

Heather's face flashed in my head the way it had in that video: her hair pulled back, bare feet on our cabin's wood floor, moving like she belonged there. I thought about the photographs I had seen of her since I'd only met her once, as Heather Evans once.

She'd looked like a younger version of me, although I hadn't seen it then, but maybe I was just letting myself believe that.

The videos from the security camera had been checked out. Emily's investigator had scrubbed the metadata until it showed its truth: real timestamps, real depth-of-field changes, the small warp of the lens we always got when the camera caught the water's brightness through the sliders. But a part of it was amiss.

The audio. That was a lie.

Braden's voice on the clip saying, "You're going to love this place," the words that had made me sick when I'd first heard them, came on a separate track. They had been dropped into the video track using Adobe Premiere Pro video editing software with a lazy hand and the assumption we'd never look at the meta data. But the investigator had. He'd circled it in his report: a synthetic timbre, the tiniest smear on a consonant where the model interpolated what it didn't have. It was Braden's voice, but it was fake. The investigator explained: "With a few seconds of a clean capture recording of someone's voice, anyone could easily clone it with software.

She could have fake-Braden saying anything she wanted. She could have him reading *War and Peace* if she wanted. But she kept it short and not too incriminating. A much more effective mindfuck against me.

It would have been easy for Heather to record Braden at work without him even knowing. A few seconds were all she would need.

But the video part, that was real. So there was no doubt Heather had been in our cabin. She had created that smart-lock code and gone up there when we were absent. To set this up. To snoop into our lives—I don't know. But she was there.

She obviously knew every move we made, so she would know the cabin was empty. A perfect place to hide out with Lucy.

Heather had walked the same boards where Lucy had learned to toddle. She'd stood at the same sink where I'd rinsed sand out of tiny swimsuits, snow from shoes. She'd opened our cabinets. She'd looked out our windows at the water and the trees and the black ribbon of dock.

Where else would she run now?

The road curved and started to climb for real. A convoy of 18-wheeler trucks huffed and settled into their lanes.

I should have called Emily again. I should have called Braden. Instead, I ignored their calls and text messages.

I should have called anyone. But I'd killed the tracking on my phone hours ago because I couldn't stand the idea of red-and-blue in my rearview and questions I didn't want to answer until Lucy was in my arms. I told myself I was buying time, not cutting myself off. I told myself a lot of things.

The sign for DONNER SUMMIT slid by. My ears popped with the change in air pressure. I cracked the window and let a blade of cold in. It woke me up in a way coffee never did. The smell was resin and something metallic, like snow that hadn't fallen yet.

My mind kept trying to take inventory, so I let it. Flashlight in the glove box. Phone charging. Gas a little over half-tank. A granola bar I'd found under a pack of wipes in the door pocket. One jacket. Sneakers on my feet. No plan except getting there and opening a door.

I didn't let myself picture what I might find inside.

Every time I tried, Lucy's face filled the space. How her cheek felt when she fell asleep in the car and I carried her in. The unsteady laugh she had the night she lost her first tooth, surprised by her own body. The way she looked when she lied about brushing, telling on herself with mint breath and dry toothbrush.

Heather's face pressed in behind Lucy's. I'd never seen the newborn I'd delivered become a toddler, then a little girl, then someone who had to teach herself how to armor. I'd only seen the last version: weaponized. The one that had shot and killed the man who had abused her. I hadn't given her a name. Someone else had. Others had raised her until they died, and then the state foster system had ruined her. And here we were.

The turnoff towards the cabin came quickly. I eased onto the narrower road that threaded the hill, down towards the waterfront, a familiar sequence of turns my body knew better than my head. The houses were spaced out, vast homes overlooking the water, made to look like old-time log cabins.

I turned into a tree-lined road that led to our driveway. I swallowed hard and pulled deeper into the pocket of trees that held our place.

The cabin sat above the waterline, surrounded by the forest, not a neighbor in sight.

A place built for quiet. Long metal sticks that served as snow markers during winters swayed in the breeze.

I pulled up to the garage but didn't open it. I cut the engine and listened. The cooling tick of the hood as the over-worked engine settled. The small separate sounds of the forest —the skinny chatter of a bird, a branch falling somewhere out of sight. No other cars. No voices. No laughter. No crying.

Tucking the phone in my pocket, I got out. Cold climbed up my shins. The air made my lungs snap. I stood still and let my eyes adjust to the high elevation. The water was a dark plate behind the trees. The sky had gone thin, and the last light punched to the west.

Emily would have told me to wait. Braden would have

begged me to wait, to not go inside. The police would have told me to stand by for a unit.

Yet I took the path that cut between manzanita and pine, the one where Lucy ran barefoot even when I told her not to. Needles cushioned the ground. A squirrel's cry went off like a cheap alarm to my right and I stopped, heart banging, then forced myself forward. The deck boards gave a little under my weight with their old familiar groan. My hand found the rail where Lucy had carved a heart we'd told her not to. I pressed my thumb into the shallow shape until it hurt.

The front door was in shadow. I stood there long enough to feel stupid. Long enough to hear my own breath turn into something I didn't recognize. I tested the knob because that's what you do even when you know you shouldn't.

Locked.

My finger shook—not from the cold—as I entered the code into the smart-lock keypad.

The hinge squealed because I never remembered to oil it until I heard it groan. That sound felt too loud, and for a second I waited for someone inside to answer it. No answer came.

I pushed the door an inch and stopped. House noises or footsteps? Wind or breath? The table, the couch, the copper pan that always doubled the light.

"Heather?" It came out too soft. The word vanished into the room.

I eased the door wider, feeling like a burglar in my own home.

Then I stepped in. In the glass of the sliding door, a small figure flickered beside mine—brown hair, a narrow shoulder.

The world tilted. "Lucy!"

THIRTY-ONE

"LUCY! SWEETHEART!"

My words bounced off the glass and came back as an empty echo. The small figure by the slider flickered, then resolved into what it was: my own reflection doubled in the pane beside Lucy's red jacket on the peg by the door, behind me. Brown hair. A narrow shoulder. Me.

Not her.

The air left me in a small, stupid sound I'd never made before. I pressed a hand to the doorframe because the room seemed to shift a degree to the left.

"Okay," I said to no one. "Okay."

I made my way through the house. The couch was empty, the throw folded wrong in the way I always hated and never fixed. The kitchen was clean except for the blue enamel mug by the sink and a faint ring of water like a map that didn't lead anywhere. I touched the mug—cold. Meaningless. My heart insisted otherwise.

"Lucy?" I tried again, more loudly. "Heather?"

Nothing. The house absorbed the names and didn't give them back.

Opening the hall closet, I stared at stacks of beach towels, board games with pieces missing, and the box of Christmas lights we never remembered to test until December. I checked the bathroom, its damp, metallic smell of old pipes and pine cleaner. I lifted the shower curtain and hated myself for hoping I would find her there.

Upstairs, in Lucy's bedroom, I flicked on the light. Empty. Lucy's bed was made. No dent in the pillow. The only thing looking back at me was a nine-square Taylor Swift collage of butterflies, hearts, *Shake It Off* in neon, and the singer's silhouette with a guitar. The glossy paper caught my gaze and threw it back in a taunt. Everything was like I had left it the last time we were here. I still continued my search.

Bedroom two: the spare. Nice and tidy. Nothing out of place, which suddenly felt like the most accusing thing in the world.

I checked under the beds because grief makes you ridiculous. I used my cell phone flashlight, the beam catching dust and a wad of Sunny's fur. The need for a better cleaning service somehow popped in my head as I stood up.

Next, I checked our room. Big and ridiculously opulent, all of a sudden. The walk-in closet yawned like a small store; rows of shoes in tidy ranks, silk and wool asleep on their hangers. In the bath, the marble his-and-hers gleamed, twin bowls waiting for faces that weren't here. The shower with two heads smelled faintly of eucalyptus; the Waterworks tub for two sat in the corner by the floor-to-ceiling window framing the pines and the lake, like a postcard someone had forgotten to send. No glass on the counter. No towel out of place.

No one was here, and no one had been here lately.

Downstairs, the other spare bedroom was turned down as if in a hotel that had lost its guest. The posh family room —cashmere throw, designer coffee-table books—looked staged instead of lived in. Pantry: neat rows of canned goods and mason jars, everything labeled. Wine cellar: cool air, sleeping bottles. The three-car garage: empty slots, epoxy gleaming where the Cayenne should be.

I ran outside. The pool wore its winter lid, taut and silent. The built-in grill gleamed under its cover. The changing room smelled like chlorine and cedar, towels folded with military precision. All of it expensive. All of it useless.

No voices. No footsteps. Just wind in the trees and the lake ticking against the dock.

I went back inside and the house felt larger on the way in than it had on the way out. The edges of the hallway softened. A creeping wooziness climbed behind my eyes, and I put a hand to the wall to steady the tilt.

They weren't here.

The certainty came in like a tide and took all my strength with it. I closed the slider door and leaned my forehead against the cold glass until it bit. My breath fogged and disappeared, fogged and disappeared, as if I was practicing vanishing.

I had been so sure that they'd be here.

My legs felt like they were going to fold under me and I sat at the table, then I stood because sitting felt like surrender. I walked a slow circuit I'd walked a hundred times—front door, kitchen, hall, bedrooms, back to the sliding patio door—as if a loop might produce different results should I thread it enough.

Then a feeling of dread. What if they weren't headed north at all? The thought opened like a trapdoor under me.

When Heather switched cars in Novato, she could have just as easily gone south instead of north. She could be closing in on Bakersfield by now with Lucy. Or she could be headed towards the East Coast.

My so-called motherly instinct was a joke that falsely assured me she would be here. It was a cruel hoax.

I checked my watch. By the time I made it back down the mountain and back to Vista Bay, she could be clearing Los Angeles. Another couple hours from there and she'd be near San Diego and the Mexican border.

"No," I said, like it mattered to say it out loud.

But the calculations insisted on happening. The map unrolled in my head, distances and times stacking, my three hours up here already a loss I couldn't get back. Every minute I stood in this empty house could be another ten miles between her and me. Lucy strapped into a seat, staring straight ahead because that's what kids do when they're trying not to cry. Wondering where I was. And what was Heather telling her? That they were sisters. That I had abandoned Lucy, like I had Heather.

I tasted metal. I swallowed hard and it didn't change. My pulse had migrated to my mouth, my wrists, the soft places at my temples. I hadn't eaten much. That old granola bar in the car that had tasted like cardboard and disappeared before I knew I'd opened it. Water, a little. Altitude and fear were doing their worst to my body.

What should I do? Run out of here, jump in my car, and drive more than three hours back to Vista Bay? Call the police? And tell them what? No one broke into my cabin. No one is here.

"Think," I told myself, feeling the room spinning.

Make a list. Call Emily. Call Braden. Call the police. Turn the tracking back on. Give them the address. Tell them I'd been wrong. Let them come sweep the place with flashlights and competence. Stand on the deck and listen for a boat that wasn't coming. Drive south, now, tonight. Gas. Bathroom. Keys. Shoes.

All these thoughts kept crashing though me all at once.

I put my hand on the table to steady the paper for note taking and realized there was no paper, just wood under my palm and my hand shaking. I sat again and the room spun. I went out to the deck.

With my eyes closed, I saw Lucy at age three, sticky with marshmallows and on the exact patch of deck where I was standing, her hair blown into her mouth and her laughter catching there. I saw her at ten, cross-armed and indignant when I said to put on a sweater even though "it's not cold, Mom." I then saw a baby with damp, matted, thin brown hair I never named being carried away from me, the whole world narrowing to a doorframe and a pair of hands that weren't mine.

"Stop," I told the ghosts. They didn't.

Inside, the floor slipped sideways. My phone clattered across the boards and bounced near the wall. I bent to grab it and the room slid again, a raft in rough water I hadn't seen coming. The ringing in my ears—had it been there before?—grew until it was a thread pulling through everything.

Panic surged from the center of my being and burst outward; my chest burned, my breath snagged. It felt like I was dying. A heart attack?

Breathe slower. Count. In through your nose, out. Nice and steady.

I sat. I stood. I couldn't decide which would break me less.

In the corner of my eye, Lucy's red jacket—the one we'd left here the last time we came as a family. I reached for it as if it was a lifeline and pressed it tight to my chest, into my face, inhaling hard, trying to catch what was left of her.

"Lucy... where are you?" I said between ragged breaths.

The last thing I felt was the floor rising to meet me and the cold boards against my cheek as my vision faded.

Then the lights went out.

THIRTY-TWO

"She was not part of the plan," Monalisa said, chin jutting toward the loft upstairs where I'd locked Lucy. Her voice was low, furious.

"You don't have to whisper. I gave her another shot. She's in la-la land."

"Another one? Jesus, you're going to OD her with all that milk you keep giving her. She's tiny," Monalisa said, referring to the propofol I was using to keep the little princess knocked out by its street name: *milk of amnesia.*

"I have this under control." I felt annoyed she was questioning me like I was a moron.

"Do you? Because she's not supposed to be here!" she said, getting louder. "The plan was to blow up your mother's perfect life and drain their bank account, not kidnapping."

"She's not my *mother.*" I felt my disdain on my tongue.

"You know what I mean," Monalisa snapped back.

I shrugged.

"I had to pivot," I said, keeping my tone flat.

"Pivot? You kidnapped a fucking child. A rich little white girl. Cops will lose their shit over that, and the media will be lining up at the trough to feast off a story like this. Her face will be everywhere faster than you can say 207A."

That was the California penal code for kidnapping. We could recite the criminal penal code better than most public defense lawyers. It was one of Monalisa's things. *Know your enemy.* She was obsessed with Sun Tzu and quoted him often. *If you know the enemy and know yourself, you need not fear the result of a hundred battles.* She even had a tattoo on her wrist in Chinese calligraphy characters that spelled out his name: 孫子.

I shrugged. "That plan failed. She took Braden back. They were on their way back to being that nauseating picture-perfect family again. And they lawyered up with a real pit bull of an attorney, so our plan crumbled. I didn't go through all this to just let them carry on like before. So I hit her where it really hurts. Her precious little daughter. The one she didn't throw away."

Monalisa stared me down, both eyes blown wide, a look of amusement on her face. "Damn, girl. I should be getting angrier with this stunt you pulled, but I'll be honest —I'm impressed with your cojones."

The corner of my mouth slipped up. She didn't smile back.

"So what's the end game now?" she said.

I bit the inside of my cheek. I'd been chewing that question since I'd pulled out of the school's parking lot. "I want her kid to walk in my shoes."

A blink. "How?"

"You're connected. Your people pay for that kind of merchandise," I said, looking upstairs towards the attic room.

She whistled, slowly and softly. "Jesus, Ash. Your own little sister?"

"Half-sister," I corrected her. "And I was a kid. I survived. She can too." I sighed.

"Not everyone does."

Why was she so concerned about that spoiled brat? I could always count on her being a stone-cold gangster. Was it because the girl was my half-sister? Did that make me colder? *Screw it.*

"You're missing the point. Jenna will never come back from this. Not from losing the one she loves."

Now Monalisa looked at me as if she didn't recognize me. She'd always thought she knew me—but she didn't know me. She'd only thought she did because I'd shown the part of me I wanted her to see. That was it.

"Can you help me," I asked, "or not?"

She didn't make me wait. "You know I've had your back since we were kids." A beat. "I'll help."

THE FIRST TIME she told me the future belonged to the one who could read the current before it formed a wave, I was fifteen and she was sixteen. She always liked to wax philosophical after lights out, even back then. It's how she became the top dog in juvie. She always saw the big picture. And she was fearless. No one could intimidate her. Inmates. COs. the warden. Nobody.

She had told me that once she was on the outside, she saw the future was not street hustling or gang banging, a male-dominated world anyways. She had traded those corners for computer screens. She loved to refer to her cell phone as her own personal ATM. She might have been off the street, but she was always hustling. 24/7. ABH, she loved to say with a smirk. Instead of the old sales mantra from *Glengarry Glen Ross*, ABC, or always be closing, it was: always be hustling, ABH.

But she'd shifted her hustle.

"Why work a block for chump change," she said, "when you can skim the whole world from behind a computer screen—and skip the turf wars and all that shit?"

She hooked up with a washed-up Russian mobster living in West Hollywood who ran complex frauds, human trafficking, and cybercrime—the last of which Monalisa was hungry to learn. She learned fast. Then she went out on her own.

Monalisa ran crews across time zones, ghosts who spoke in handles, not names. In places where money moved without hands. Encrypted messages burned as soon as they were read. No sirens if you were careful. No informants unless you were sloppy.

Three years after I got out, she found me. She showed up at my crappy apartment in a pimped-out Escalade. She hugged me tightly; I returned the hug, giving her back what she wanted.

"If you're with me," she said, "you won't go hungry again."

I wasn't hunting cash. I was hunting a ghost. I knew right away that Monalisa could help me find them. The ones who dumped me at birth like garbage out on the curve.

Why I was so set on finding them? They'd given me up, after all. It was probably ingrained in the DNA of those who had been put up for adoption. For what reason? And who were my real parents?

It was no different for me. I wanted to find them.

No information had been given to me about my biological relatives. All I had was my adopted parents' files, but they were heavily redacted when it came to details about my birth parents.

But that didn't seem to slow down Monalisa's geeks, as

she called them.

A week later, she sent me a link. She warned me before clicking it. "Are you sure you want what you think you want?"

I was, so I clicked. I poured over every document hunched over my laptop until my back screamed.

My father had died in Afghanistan, 2003. My mother was alive and thriving. Not the woman I imagined (broken, surviving, waiting for rescue), but the kind whose registry listed Matouk and Le Creuset; the kind who'd married into one of the richest families in California; the kind who stared at the bay from a house so high on top of the world that the fog looked like a rug below her.

Literally on top of the world looking down at me. Did she ever wonder if I was down there, somewhere?

The amount of documents were voluminous. Property records in San Francisco and Marin County. A wedding announcement. A college transcript. A fancy law firm announcing a promotion to partner. Wedding pictures.

And there she was. All smiles. White teeth, white flowers. More pictures: a black-tie gala to *benefit kids in crisis*. Cute. And a photo of a gap-toothed girl holding a strawberry bigger than her face.

Jenna. Braden. Lucy. Even a dog. I was certain there was a white picket fence somewhere nearby. The perfect family.

A rage surged inside me. It wasn't just that they were happy. It was that their happiness left no space for me.

I'd spent years looking for her only to get slammed against the brick wall of a closed adoption. One click, and Monalisa's Romanian computer hacker geek pulled the wall down like it was made of thin paper.

"Was it hard to get this stuff?" I'd asked her.

"Like taking candy from a baby," she'd said.

The more I learned about her, the hotter my disdain burned.

At first, all my stalking was done online. But eventually, you have to be up close and personal. Like an addiction that keeps escalating. I moved up to Northern California.

Vista Bay security was a joke. Rich pricks in LA lived in gated communities but not in the San Francisco Bay. No real gate. A few cameras, but nothing to fret over. A dog that barked for attention, not warning.

I wasn't sure how I would feel the first time I saw her in person. I didn't plan to show myself to her. But would I change my mind once I saw her? Would I walk up to her, and say, "Mom?"

But I stood outside their home in the dark, and I watched her through those big floor-to-ceiling windows with the daughter she loved, the one she'd kept. Bile climbed my throat. I spat, swallowed hard. She was going to pay for what she had done to me.

. . .

JENNA'S LIFE ran on a loop: house → school → errands → gym → pickup → home. I learned the rhythm of her breathing, then I reinvented myself.

Heather Evans. Paralegal because that would be the perfect way of entwining myself into their lives. The certificate program was a breeze.

The job came down to me and one other. I asked for Monalisa's help. "No problem," she said.

Two days later, some vile social media postings from my competitor from years ago popped up. I got the job.

Once inside Braden's firm, I needed to get even closer to him. My stepdad, I giggled. I had to get rid of his paralegal so I could step in. Monalisa once again came through from Romania with love. Photographs and videos no decent person should ever have on their work computer. It was ugly business, but he was in my way. Then he wasn't.

From there, it was the slow burn I'm good at, and I began to tear away at Braden's privileged life. A mislabeled file. The wrong calendar nudge. Critical documents deleted from the server as if they'd never existed. Pretending to run into him at Niza Cafe with Monalisa plus a long-lens camera waiting across the street. Rumors dressed as concerns.

People think reputations explode. Most of the time, it's a slow rot until the footing gives way.

The cabin clip was a different kind of knife: my birth mother's space, my body in it, and a voice that would make her bleed. We recorded the house for real. Monalisa's guy handled the rest. All I had to do was email a one-minute clip of Braden's voice, which I recorded at work, and I could have him say anything I wanted. But subtlety and restraint were key here to really mess with Jenna's head.

Then it was time for me to Meryl-up and put in a stellar performance for HR.

The restraining order. The suit. Grain by grain, I salted her life.

But even a well-planned and perfectly executed plan goes to shit. After my six months of slowly chipping away at the perfect family's foundation, they pulled back together before it could crumble, permanently.

So I had to improvise. Why didn't Monalisa see that? I had no other choice. She was helping me, because she loved me, but I knew she wasn't happy with the kidnapping.

"If we're doing this, we do it fast and smart," Monalisa said, pulling me back from my memories. "We don't keep the heat."

She made calls I won't describe. One voice on the third ring felt like oil. He said he had room for that sort of package. He could make a girl like Lucy vanish. "No problem." he hissed.

That night Monalisa leaned on the counter, arms folded. "We're at the point of no return."

"I know," I said. "When do you hand her over?"

"I said I know someone who knows someone. I didn't say I'd feed him your sister."

"Half," I corrected again.

She blinked. "You want that done, *you* hand her over."

We stared at each other until the air thinned. "Help me," I said.

She always caved. Starved love bends.

"You know I will."

I smiled and gave her the doe-eyed look she liked. "When?"

"It's already in motion. But it takes time. A few days."

Great. Babysitting the princess longer than I'd planned.

"We watch her closely," Monalisa added, like she could hear me thinking. "If she gets out, it's over for both of us."

No shit. I thought, but didn't say that out loud.. "I got it, babe," I said instead. She liked it when I slid into lovey-dovey, happy-couple mode. Despite being a tough, hardened gangster, Monalisa was as easy to hustle as anyone. Prison had taught me the trick: Everybody has a soft spot. Find it. Press at will.

. . .

MONALISA RAN into town to pick up groceries when my burner buzzed. Motion alert—Morrissey Tahoe cabin.

I pulled up the feed. Jenna. I thumbed on audio and heard her calling for Lucy, voice raw, bouncing off their pretty wood and stone as she made her way through the cabin like a banshee.

I rubbed the thin scar on my wrist, the old ache pulsing to life. Of course she would. She would come looking for her.

Of course she would. She would come looking for her.

How'd she land on Tahoe? I was impressed. The sedan I'd taken after ditching the Cayenne didn't point to me or this address.

The outdoor camera showed she was alone. No sirens, no Braden—just Jenna on instinct. That tracked. Unlike for me, she'd do anything for the daughter she didn't leave behind.

The feed jittered—pixel snow, audio a half-second behind. Jenna swept past the hallway camera, one hand on the wall, Lucy's jacket clenched to her chest like a flotation device. She blinked hard, swayed, tried to breathe herself steady.

Then she folded.

A soft, ugly thud off-frame; the lens caught the edge of her shoulder and hair as she hit the boards. The mic picked up that little empty sound people make when the lights go out.

I scrubbed back and watched it again. And again.

The clip looped; the thrill smoothed into something calmer, cleaner. I smiled and let it stay.

THIRTY-THREE

My phone vibrated against the hardwood floor. For a second, I didn't know where I was, only that the boards under my cheek were cold and the room smelled like dust and old pine. The jacket was still in my arms. Lucy's jacket. I'd pulled it up like oxygen, right before I blacked out. Memory hit and I pushed up too fast; the room spun.

The phone kept ringing.

I found the phone by sound. BRADEN. I thumbed it open.

"Jenna?" His tone was tight, careful. "You there?"

"I'm here," I said, and heard how unconvincing that sounded.

"You were right," he said. "About Tahoe. About going north."

I closed my eyes. "No. I was wrong. She's not here. No one's been in the cabin."

"No, you were right. Emily's guy found a place. Near Incline Village."

Incline Village was just over the Nevada line, not even twenty miles from here. "How?"

"Two things. First, the harassing messages you've been getting, one had a shortened link. The PI pulled the redirect logs. The hit came from a public IP at the Starbucks in Incline Village. She got sloppy and used their Wi-Fi."

That was days ago. Even if it was Heather then, it didn't mean she had stayed here.

"There's more," Braden said, slipping into that infomercial cadence he gets when he's trying not to get ahead of himself. "There was an Instagram post from Ryan Kim." I could hear Braden's voice dip recalling the punch, but he recovered. "It was from months ago, posted about a weekend at a cabin in Lake Tahoe with a tag to Heather's account."

Heather's Finsta account, I thought as Braden continued. "The PI ran a visual match of the tree line, roof angles against cached listing photos. Zillow, Redfin, old Airbnb mirrors, he scoured them all with a nifty crawling program. He found a pulled listing with cedar siding and a half-moon window just like the one in Ryan's photograph."

My blood went cold and hot at the same time. "That can't be enough to get an address."

"It wasn't. But it narrowed it down to four A-frame cabins near Incline Village. Only one wasn't on any short-term sites any longer. Zillow shows it listed for rent, now marked 'unavailable.' The PI called a contact at a Nevada tenant-screening agency. And he hit paydirt. Active lease. Jennifer Anderson."

"Who's that?" I asked.

"The PI's contact sent him a copy from the application form that included a copy of Jennifer Anderson's driver's license. It's her. It's Heather."

The room tilted again; I had to sit. "You have an address."

"Yes." Paper shuffled. "32 Ponderosa Spur. Emily already passed it to the police. They're rolling units from both jurisdictions. She told me to tell you to stay put. Do not go there. She's dangerous, honey."

Even more reason to go now.

"Jenna—"

"I'm not staying here." I sounded steady. I didn't feel steady.

Silence. I could hear him breathing. "I'm heading to Gnoss Field. Charter's wheels up in twenty; I can be at Truckee–Tahoe airport in about forty-five minutes. Please wait for me; we'll go together."

"Lucy doesn't have forty-five minutes," I said as I hung up the phone. I headed out the door. The night met me with a bite. As I got into the car, I noticed I was still holding onto Lucy's jacket. I held it tightly, then gently put it down on the passenger seat.

The engine turned over and the dash turned my hands a sickly blue. Quarter tank. More than enough. I didn't want to stop. Not for anything.

I plugged the address Braden gave me into the GPS and watched the route snake along the north shore like a thin blue vein. Fourteen miles around the lake, through Kings Beach, into Crystal Bay, across the state line into Nevada, then down to the turnoff and a stretch of road where the cabin Heather had rented as Jennifer Johnson was located. At this time, traffic would be light. I would be there in less than twenty minutes. *Hold on, Lucy.*

Headlights sliced the trees into ribs as I pulled onto the road. The lake to my right was iron under a thin skin of wind, the shoreline a dotted necklace of porch lights and empty decks. The car's steady hum filled the cabin, a low thread under the wind's rush and the whisper of tires on asphalt.

"Call Emily," I told myself, and didn't. I didn't want another voice telling me to wait. I rolled my shoulders and kept my eyes on the pale paint of the centerline, tunnel-visioning my way east.

The road began to lean and curve in the kind of mountain S-turns you feel in your molars. A sign flashed past: ICY PATCHES POSSIBLE. Luckily, we were a couple of months from the first snowfall. That was the last thing I needed right now, trying to drive through the mountain with snow in the picture.

I eased a degree off the gas at a wide turn with only a thin aluminum guardrail between me and a steep ravine.

Kings Beach came quickly; I squeezed the wheel and passed through the town. It was quiet. I didn't see any signs of the police rolling out to the cabin. I knew the area was covered by the Placer County Sheriff's Office, and they had a large jurisdiction in Lake Tahoe up to the Nevada state line. There was no way I was going to sit and wait at our cabin for them to mobilize.

My phone pinged. A text notification from Emily: *Wait for the police. Do not approach the structure.* It was as if she had read my mind.

A second later a notification popped up on my phone: *Share location with Emily Acosta.* I stared at the button long enough to feel stupid and hit *Share.* If I went missing, at least she would be able to relay my location to the police.

As I drove, two sets of yellow eyes flashed in the brush and then broke onto the road—a doe and her fawn at the last second. I braked, heart in my throat. We held each other's gaze for two beats—two protective mothers—before she sprang into the trees on pogo-stick legs, the fawn close behind, and they vanished into the dark.

I exhaled, eased the wheel straight, and pressed the accelerator. My hand found Lucy's jacket on the passenger seat. "I'm coming, baby," I said.

THIRTY-FOUR

I watched Jenna drop to the floor a few more times on my phone.

Each time, it got funnier.

It was almost poetic.

When headlights swept across the front window, I grabbed my phone. Monalisa's Raptor Jeep crunched to a stop outside. The slam of the driver's door came next, followed by the crunch of pine needles under her Prada platform boots as she made her way to the door.

The cabin door creaked open. Cold air mixed with the fruity haze of her vape came in first, then her.

We were the same height, but those boots made her tower over me.

She dropped a grocery bag on the counter.

"You're not gonna believe the circus at the store," she

said. "The boomer in front of me was trying to pay with change. Who does that nowadays? Took forever—"

She stopped mid-sentence when she saw my face.

"What?" she asked. "What happened?"

I picked up my phone and showed her. "You'll want to sit for this."

She came closer. I hit play.

Jenna appeared on the tiny screen, moving through her cabin, calling Lucy's name. Monalisa's eyes widened. When Jenna collapsed, she gasped and clapped a hand over her mouth.

"Oh my God," she whispered. "She's here? She found us?"

"She's here," I said, setting the phone on the table.

"What the hell happened to her?"

"Nothing. She passed out. She gets up after a while."

Monalisa's face darkened. "What the hell, Ash. We need to split."

"Calm down. She's alone. No cops. No husband. Just her."

"That's worse!" Her voice jumped. "That means she's desperate. If she's here, it's not an accident. She's onto us."

"She's not onto anything," I said. "It's a lucky guess, that's all. She doesn't know about this cabin. It's rented under a fake name. She can't trace us."

"She's like ten miles away! That's not nothing."

"More like twenty." I leaned back in the chair, folding

my arms. Monalisa glared at me. "Relax. She'll leave by morning. She came here chasing ghosts. She always does."

Monalisa started pacing, sucking on her vape, arms crossed tight. "This has gone too far. It's out of control."

"Nothing's out of control," I said. "The rendezvous is set. Your contact's expecting us at the motel in Reno two nights from now. We just need to stay put."

Her head snapped toward me. "Two days? Are you nuts? We need to pack and go now. Just leave the kid. We vanish."

"Leave the kid?" My laugh was sharp and humorless. "That's your solution?"

"It's the only one that doesn't end with us in prison for a decade or two." She pressed a hand to her forehead. "We walk away. Tonight. Go lay low somewhere far away. Like Portugal or Spain. Before this whole thing goes up in smoke."

"It's not going up in smoke."

"Ash, listen to yourself. She's in town. She's here. And you want to sit tight for two days?"

"She doesn't know we're here."

"She didn't drive 200 miles for shits and giggles," Monalisa said. "She'll find us. You keep underestimating her."

I stood, more slowly than I needed to, because I didn't like the feeling of her towering over me. "I don't underestimate anyone. Especially not her."

"That woman is so in your head that you don't see it, and you're getting sloppy, reckless. And that's how people get caught."

"She. Is not. In my head," I said, furious that she would say that to me.

"Then prove it. Let's leave. Now, please."

"Nothing changes."

She stopped pacing. "What?"

"Nothing changes," I repeated, evenly this time. "The plan stands."

Monalisa let out a soft, incredulous laugh. "You really think you're still in charge, don't you?"

"I know I am."

Her eyes shimmered in the low light, not with fear this time but with anger. "You think this is control? It's not. It's an obsession. You're addicted to her. I'm begging you, let's go."

"Careful," I said quietly. "You're starting to sound soft."

She threw up her hands. "You have some serious mommy issues, Ash. This is insane. I'm not doing this. I was already having second thoughts about handing a ten-year-old girl to those men. Not for you, not for anyone."

"She's not just some girl. She's Jenna's blood."

"Your blood too."

"That didn't mean shit to Jenna when she gave me up. Why should I care?"

"She's a kid. Like we were in juvie. That's what you want for her?"

"It makes it justice."

"No, Heather." She'd stopped using my real name and looked mournful. "It makes it pathetic."

That one landed harder than I wanted to admit. I made sure she couldn't see it.

I moved to the counter and started stacking the cans she'd brought in—beans, soup, bottled water. Busy hands. Calm tone. "You done?"

Monalisa's laugh was hollow this time. "I'm not going down in flames over nothing."

"Over nothing?" I turned. "I was left to be—"

"Get over it!" she snapped. The words hit like a slap. "You're not the only one who had a shitty childhood. I was abused as a kid every day and twice on Sunday. You don't see me out here crying over spilt milk. I used it. I got stronger. I moved on."

I stared at her. "Spare me the Tony Robbins bullshit."

She took a shaky breath. "You said you always wanted someone who had your back. I've always had it. I still do. That's why I'm telling you. We need to go. Now."

"No."

"Then I'm not going down with you for this. You want to hand a kid over to those animals because your mother didn't love you? You go right ahead. But I'm not sticking around to watch it."

"Don't call her my mother."

"I'll do whatever I want," she said. "You don't own me."

"Are you sure about that?"

Her eyes flashed, wet and furious. "Yeah. I am."

She turned and crossed to the bedroom, grabbed her go-bag from the closet. The zipper sounded loud in the small cabin. She slung it over her shoulder and faced me. For the first time in years, she looked like someone who might actually walk away.

"You're making a mistake," I said.

"I've made plenty," she said. "Staying with you was one of them."

She double-timed it from the bedroom to the front door without looking at me. Once there, she hesitated. "Come with me," she said quietly, not turning around. "Please."

I didn't answer. She turned to look at me. Her eyes were red and puffy. Cheeks wet. I just stared back. If she expected tears from me, she was sorely mistaken. It was all she needed to know, as if the reality of our relationship suddenly dawned on her.

Her jaw tightened. She was trying to stay hard, but the tears came anyway. "I thought you cared about me," she said.

"I did. Until you stopped being useful."

Her expression went still, like a lake freezing over. She shook her head, turned around, opened the door and left.

THIRTY-FIVE

As I made my way down State Route 28—a state highway that travels along the northern shore of Lake Tahoe—I couldn't stop thinking how we had driven these roads for years as a family. I couldn't even hazard a guess at the number of times we'd taken these same roads. A hundred times? Thousands? More?

It hurt because good memories crept in, but my sense of dread about what was happening to Lucy wouldn't allow those pleasant thoughts to linger long.

I wiped a tear trickling down my cheek with the back of my hand. I need to stay strong. I hoped against hope that Lucy was there. My gut told me yes, my brain told me not to get my hopes high. I'd thought I would find her at our cabin, and I was wrong.

She might not even be in the area. *She might be dead...*

"Stop," I yelled out loud, though I was the only person in the car.

I drove along the lake crossing the California-Nevada border and into Incline Village. It was a short drive, but it felt too long as my sweaty palms gripped the steering wheel tightly.

Up here, night came with a thickness you don't get in the city. There are few streetlights, and cabins are buried deep in the trees. The road ran through a kind of manufactured blackness that provoked chills on an ordinary evening; tonight it felt sentient. The Cayenne's adaptive headlights kept swiveling, cutting and brightening as the road bent—white blades slicing the dark, making new shadows faster than they cleared the old ones. A handful of cars were on the road, their drivers oblivious to what was going on. I envied them.

I was almost at the cabin when my phone buzzed, the sudden burst of brightness from the screen making my eyes squint.

The car's dashboard screen said, *Unknown Caller,* but I knew who was calling. She wasn't unknown. I should've let it die in silence, but I couldn't do that. I took the call without saying anything.

"Hello there," a woman said. Calm. Pleased with herself. "Nice night for a drive." The edge in her voice made me shudder. I had no doubt that she had been tracking us for a very long time; she knew where I was, and where I was headed.

"Ashley," I said, using Heather's real name. The name given to her by her adoptive parents, not me.

"Good. We're done pretending. But my name is Heather now."

"Where is my daughter?"

A beat. Then, cold and cutting: "I'm right here."

The line carried my own breath back to me. Guilt hit like a stomach punch. She was right, in the worst way. I gave birth to a child and then signed her away to strangers. My mother had been teary-eyed and distant, unable to look at the granddaughter she was also surrendering. My father was disgusted and nowhere to be seen.

"Heather, listen to me."

My voice shook and I let it. I couldn't put up a charade; Heather knew that I was on the verge of a nervous breakdown. It was why she'd taken Lucy. It was why she had destroyed Braden's reputation. To hurt me.

"Whatever you want. Money, a clean start, I will make it happen. I won't cooperate with the police. I won't press charges. The Morrissey family can wire you enough money to disappear well and permanently. Just bring Lucy to me."

She scoffed. "You think I did all this for money? I have money. I can buy a dozen names and three new faces before breakfast. I don't need your fucking money. This was never about that."

"It's about me." The words scraped. "I'm sorry for what you went through. I—"

"Save it. You never came looking, even after you got rich. You never told a soul about me. Not even your husband. Not your precious daughter. My own sister. I watched you for months pretending to be a good mother. Made me sick."

"I was sixteen," I said. "I was afraid, and my father gave me no choice. They told me you were safe. In a good home. I told myself you had a better life without me. It was a lie I lived with every day."

"Excuses, excuses," Heather said. I could feel the hatred she had for me reverberating through the call.

"Please. Take me instead. Do whatever you came here to do, but let Lucy go. She's ten. She's—"

"Innocent?" Heather's tone softened into something worse than anger. "Being a child doesn't buy you anything where I grew up. You left me to the wolves and learned to sleep fine. Now your other daughter gets to learn too."

"Please. I am begging you."

"You don't get to be a good mother to her now. Not after what you did to me."

The line clicked dead.

I stared at the empty screen until the road curved under me and forced my hands back to work. The guilt stayed, heavy and all consuming. I tightened my grip and drove faster, I was so close. I was going to find my daughters.

THE GPS CHIRPED: Turn right in 0.3 miles. I slowed. The turnoff into Spur Road looked more like a long private driveway than a public road until you're on it and notice a narrow spur that climbs between manzanita and pine trees and mailboxes dotting the road. Remote. No outlet. No streetlights. Pitch black.

"You have reached your destination," the GPS announced. I was surprised it worked out here. I rolled up the incline, gravel ticking the undercarriage.

I killed the headlights before the crest and let the dark assemble itself into shapes: the split in the narrow road, the wedge of deck railings. I shut off the car. Lake Tahoe, the largest alpine lake in North America, was invisible in the darkness, but I knew it stood out there like an ominous black void beyond the trees, watching everything.

The engine ticked as it cooled. When it went quiet, my ears filled with the kind of ringing that warned of danger. I got out and walked down a patchy road.

32 *Ponderosa Spur* was stamped into a weathered post at the bend. I slid the phone to silent. I realized I was holding on to Lucy's jacket like a child clinging to its safety blanket. I shoved the jacket deep in my bag as if it could

keep me anchored and stepped off the gravel into the trees. Dry needles cracked under my boots like broken glass.

Emily's last text glowed on the lock screen: *Units en route. 20 minutes. Wait. Do not approach.*

Every word was correct. None of it felt possible, so I continued walking towards the lights that seemed to flicker among the swaying pine branch whorls.

Heather was capable of murder. She had killed her foster father. Was that what she had planned for Lucy? Or was she just using her as bait to lure me out here so she could kill me? I was okay with that, as long as she didn't hurt Lucy. All these thoughts rushed in my head like water breaking through a crumbling dam. *Keep moving forward,* I told myself. *Lucy needs you.* Heather *needs you.* That thought jarred me. But it was true. Maybe I could save my first born daughter too. Just maybe if I could get her to understand that I never stopped thinking about her. But reality bites, and deep down I knew that was just another fantasy I had conjured. She hated me. And couldn't blame her. I now knew that even as a teenage mom, I could have given her a better life than what she had to endure. But right now, I could only focus on saving Lucy.

The cabin crouched thirty yards ahead, a small A-frame cut out of the dark—cedar siding gone near black, roof line steep as a blade. It was an older cabin, one that had not yet been torn down and rebuilt into a McCabin by a rich tech bro. Through a seam in the blinds, a thin bar of light fell across the deck. I looked at the half-moon window that stared down at me like a lidless eye. I stopped to get my bearings.

There was no car in the short stretch of drive I could see. It didn't mean anything. A car could be tucked up the side. Inside the garage. A car could be anywhere. Although I couldn't see anyone, I knew there were people inside. Heather and Lucy. A screwed-up family reunion.

I flanked the drive through the pines instead of walking up it like a solicitor with a brochure and a smile. The cold had a bitter taste, like snow waiting for its cue. Somewhere down the hill, a car's headlight flashed and vanished. I wondered if that was the police.

Wait, said Emily in my head. *Do not approach. She's dangerous.*

She has Lucy, I answered in my head, and kept moving.

As I got closer, I could hear a faint hissing from the cabin, which I chalked off to regular sounds a home makes out here in the woods. I took another step closer, and in an instant the air changed. Like it had been sucked out by an intense vacuum. And in an instant it went from nighttime to day. A light so bright and warm that I couldn't make sense of what was happening as I felt immense pressure and heat, and a rolling wave that picked me up from the ground and shoved me backward like I was a rag doll.

That's when it registered. An explosion. Its blast had lifted me and set me down in the same motion like I was nothing. Deck boards bucked, then slammed. I hit the ground on my shoulder and cheek; the cold bit in a clean line. Shards of glass and wood rained down on me before the ringing in my ears drowned out all other sounds.

Once the sound came back it was muffled. I heard a horrific shout and realized it was mine. As I regained my bearings from the ground, I looked up, and the cabin seemed to have vanished into thin air.

THIRTY-SIX

THE WORLD CAME BACK IN FRAGMENTS. I COULDN'T find the strength to get up. It felt like I was lying on a playground spinner, whirling and tilting out of control.

At first there was only the ringing of my ears. A shrill, steady tone filling the hollow where sound used to live. My body registered nothing else—no weight, no pain, no air. Just that endless ringing and spinning.

Then heat rushed in. It crawled across my skin like a living thing, searing the exposed parts of my face. I opened my mouth to breathe and inhaled smoke which triggered an uncontrollable wet cough interrupted briefly by wheezing. The air was thick, heavy and sour, burning its way down my throat like I had swallowed hot coal. Something hot trickled from my nose onto my lips. Blood.

The sky wasn't black anymore. It pulsed a feverish orange, the kind of color that meant nothing good out here in wildfire country. I blinked, vision smeared and doubled, as if the world refused to settle into place.

Flames painted the tree line in streaks of orange and gold, and the air shimmered from the heat. Ash drifted down like gray snow, soft and quiet, almost beautiful—if it weren't a warning. A low wind kicked up, carrying sparks higher, scattering them into the dark like tiny flares. If this spread, the entire hillside could go up in flames.

I tried to push myself upright again, but the ground pitched beneath me. My palm slid through wet grass and splinters. Pain surged up my arm, sharp and electric. I gasped and collapsed back onto my side, blinking through the blur, giving way to another fit of phlegmy coughing. Although in pain, I finally began to regain my senses, as I looked up from my knees.

Where the cabin stood just a few minutes ago—where Lucy should have been—there was only a smoking crater. A skeletal framework of beams jutted from the rubble like ribs poking through burned flesh. The fire devoured everything in hungry crackles, flaring brighter each time it found something new to eat.

A chunk of metal was embedded into the trunk of a pine tree. Memories of the aftermath of the San Bruno pipeline explosion on television came flooding back.

My brain tried to make sense of it, but the only word that escaped through the ringing in my skull was her name.

Lucy.

It started as a whisper. Then louder.

"Lucy." I dragged myself forward, one elbow at a time, my shoulder screaming in protest. The pain radiated down my arm, but I welcomed it. It meant I was still alive.

I coughed again, harder this time, my whole chest convulsing. Every breath hurt and came with the bite of smoke. Tears burned the corners of my eyes, not from sadness, not yet, but from the fire, the heat, the impossibility of what I was seeing.

I managed to get up. The world still swayed. The night pressed down, hot and alive, the fire's roar drowning everything else out. It was surreal, like a campground bonfire that had gotten out of control.

My ears still rang, but underneath it I began to pick up other sounds; pops from burning wood, the sharp whine of something metal collapsing, distant shouting. Sirens? Or just my brain inventing noise to fill the void?

I staggered forward, my feet shuffling. The ground was littered with debris; shards of glass glittering orange, blackened boards, something that might have been a chair leg. My shoes crunched over it as I stumbled toward the flames.

"Lucy!" The scream tore itself from somewhere deep, raw and ragged, leaving my throat scorched. My legs moved before my brain could stop them. My hand reached out toward the collapsing structure, stupid and desperate. *She has to be in there. She has to be alive.*

The fire spat back at me, a burst of heat that singed my

face and forced me to stagger backward. Still, I lurched forward again, because the alternative—to do nothing—was worse.

Red and blue lights flickered across the clearing like ghosts. My vision swam as vehicles crunched up the gravel road. Doors slammed. Voices grew clearer, louder. But they were background noise. None of it mattered. Only Lucy mattered.

I stumbled closer to the fire, my lungs burning, smoke clawing its way down my throat. My shoulder throbbed with every jolt. The ground shifted beneath me, soft and unsteady from ash and splintered deck boards. Somewhere overhead, a tree branch cracked, sending a rain of embers down around me.

I didn't care.

"Lucy!" I screamed again, choking on her name this time. "Lucy, answer me!"

Nothing. Just fire. Just the infernal roar.

Then there were arms around me. Strong, rough, dragging me backward.

"Ma'am! Ma'am, you have to get back!" The voice was right in my ear, loud, but the words took a second too long to make sense. I thrashed against the grip, wild and blind. My nails scraped over rough polyester and skin.

"Let me go!" I screamed. "She's in there! She's in there!"

The man's hold tightened around my torso. "You can't go in there. It's not safe. Do you hear me? You can't."

I kicked and twisted, useless as a caught animal thrashing for freedom. "Let me *go!*"

He didn't. His boots dug into the ground behind me, his body anchoring mine as I lunged toward the inferno. The world stank of smoke and burning wood. The heat on my skin was unbearable now, as if a sun pressed too close. Tears streaked down my face—real ones now, hot trails mixing with soot and blood.

"She's in there," I whispered. The fight bled out of me as quickly as it had come. "She's in there."

"I know," the man said, his voice lower now, almost gentle. But he didn't let go.

My knees buckled. He caught me under the arms, half-carrying me back. The ground blurred past in jerks of light and shadow. Red and blue lights strobed against the trees, throwing the fire into sharper relief. Someone shouted into a radio. Another voice barked for a fire truck. It was chaotic but oddly organized. Controlled. They were already moving. They knew what to do.

I didn't. I could only watch as the cabin burned.

A raw, animal sound clawed its way out of my throat as I sagged against the man holding me. I couldn't stop it. It came from somewhere deep, where words didn't live. It echoed out into the night, swallowed by the blaze.

Some part of me registered that my hair smelled like

smoke. My face was wet with tears, sweat, and blood. My nose throbbed. My shoulder burned with pain. But none of it was real.

The only real things were the image seared into my mind, Lucy inside that cabin; my knowing no one could survive that blast; Lucy not coming out. Ever.

The man guided me farther back, beyond the immediate heat, and eased me down on the hood of a patrol car. My legs gave out before I could resist. My hands trembled as I pressed them to my face. My skin felt foreign, numb in some places, burning in others.

"She's gone," I whispered into my palms.

No one answered. Somewhere, someone shouted, "Keep back! The gas line might blow again!" More vehicles arrived. Boots pounded. Radios crackled. But all I heard were my words looping inside my head over and over again.

She's gone. She's gone. She's gone.

Every intake of breath brought more smoke. I coughed hard, chest spasming. A paramedic seemed to materialize out of nowhere and knelt beside me, hands moving gently but efficiently—checking my pulse, shining a light into my eyes. He placed a handheld oxygen mask over my nose and mouth. The clean air burned going in, but it was good— sharp and real. I barely registered his face.

"Ma'am, can you hear me? Were you inside the structure?"

I shook my head, though the world spun with the movement. "No. No, I was—she was—I should've—" My words dissolved into nothing. A sob tore loose, violent and tremulous, curling me forward. My whole body felt hollow, like something had been ripped out of me in that blast and left burning in the rubble.

The paramedic's hand rested lightly on my arm. "We're going to get you checked out, okay? You've inhaled a lot of smoke. You're in shock. Shoulder injury. Maybe a broken rib. I'm going to give you something for the pain."

Shock. Pain. The words floated past me, meaningless.

I turned my head toward the fire. Flames climbed higher, licking at the tree line now, a living monster stretching its reach. Sparks floated skyward like fireflies, drifting into the night.

The paramedic gently grabbed my arm, and jabbed it quickly, before I could notice what he was doing or protest against it. I wanted to remain alert for Lucy, but a warm, woozy wave rolled through me, softening the edges of everything. My body felt heavy, distant, as if it belonged to someone else as two paramedics slowly pushed me down onto the stretcher.

I was too far gone to fight. All I could think was that they were never going to find her. Not alive.

I began sobbing then everything turned black.

THIRTY-SEVEN

I came to slowly. Too slowly. My eyes struggled against the blinding white lights that carved the ceiling into white rectangles that would not hold still as I tried to focus.

I came up from sleep or whatever dark, heavy place where they'd put me when they sedated me, as if rising through tar. The first thing I heard was the beep. Soft, steady, indifferent. Then the rubber smell. Antiseptic threaded with smoke that wasn't here and yet somehow still in me. I realized the smoke followed me here. When I tried to swallow, the back of my throat rasped like sandpaper.

Something pinched my finger. I groggily looked down at it. A pulse oximeter. Plastic rested under my nose, feeding a whisper of cool air. My left arm lay strapped in a sling across my chest, and my right side complained when I tried to breathe too deep. My body ached in pain.

A curtain swayed at the end of the bed, its pattern of fake leaves and blue squares refusing to resolve. Someone had tucked a warmed blanket over me; it radiated comfort I didn't deserve. The sheet smelled clean. My hair did not. It reeked of smoke and night.

Lucy.

I turned my head, too fast. The room tilted left. A dull spike of pain shot through my shoulder and settled deep in the bone as if to say, *We live here now*. My rib objected to the slightest amount of pressure letting me know with an intense surge of pain. The air left me in a thin wheeze I didn't recognize as mine.

The curtain moved and a nurse in gray scrubs slid in, quiet and practiced. She sported a brown ponytail meant for business and a name badge I couldn't make focus.

Good—" She glanced at the clock. "Good evening, Jenna. I'm Erin. Can I get you some water?"

"How long have I been here?" I asked, my eyes slow to adjust.

"Two hours," the nurse said gently.

"Lucy," I said. The name came out as a scrape. "Did—" I had to breathe around the rib. "Did they find—" The rest was a cliff I couldn't make myself step off. "My daughter."

Erin's face changed in the way of people trained not to change their faces. "Let me get you that water," she said, already pouring, already moving. She slid an elevated straw to my mouth. The first sip was cold enough to sting. The second reached the dry places and made everything ache with wanting more. "Small sips. You inhaled smoke."

My eyes burned. "Lucy." It wasn't a question anymore, just a sound that filled my mouth and didn't go anywhere.

"I don't have those updates," she said gently. "The paramedics brought you in with a partial shoulder dislocation—we reduced it—a fractured rib on the right side, and a concussion. You've got minor scrapes and some smoke inhalation. But your vitals are good. The doctor will be back in a few minutes, okay?"

"I don't care." The words surprised me with their truth. "I don't care about me."

Erin rested a hand on the side rail, not touching me. "I know." She didn't. She couldn't. "The officer who came with you said a detective is on the way. He'll talk with you."

"Is she dead?" I asked. No point being brave for a stranger.

Erin's eyes flicked down, then up. "I'm so sorry, Jenna, I don't have that information."

The beeping continued, utterly bored with my apocalypse.

I looked at my hands. Black edged my nails—ash I hadn't noticed until now, packed deep as if it had grown there. A thin line of dried blood had mapped itself from my nose to my lip. Someone had cleaned most of it, but not all. My right arm bent and bunched into a sling that cut a soft diagonal from shoulder to opposite hip, neat and domestic. I wanted to tear it off and run.

"You're going to feel sore," Erin said. "We're going to manage your pain, but I need you to tell me if it spikes, okay?"

I didn't say anything.

"Can you tell me from a scale of one to ten, one feeling no pain, ten for excruciating pain, what number would you guess you're at right now?"

When I didn't answer, she asked again.

"One," I said, lying. I was in a lot of pain, but I didn't want them to knock me out with drugs. I needed to be as present as possible for Lucy.

Nurse Erin looked at me with a thin smile. She knew I was lying.

"Okay. Just let me know if the pain spikes," she said again. "You don't want to play catch up. It's best we stay ahead so we can manage it."

I deserved the pain.

"We were outside," I said to no one, to her, to the ceiling. "She was inside. I told her—" Memory bucked under me, slick and unrideable. The heat, the roar, the burst of light like a new sun. "She was inside."

Nurse Erin adjusted the cannula that fed the cool whisper to my nose. "I'll let the doctor know you're awake." Her smile could have been directed at someone whose house is burning on a television in another room. "If you need anything, press the call button."

I watched her leave as if she might unravel if I blinked. The curtain swayed closed and the room shrank. It had been painted in the sterile color every hospital chooses when it wants to be invisible. The clock's second hand jerked instead of gliding. A TV mounted near the ceiling showed ocean waves with the sound off, a screen saver pretending to be therapy.

Breathe, I told myself. The rib disliked that plan. The oxygen hissed anyway, a snake that wasn't dangerous. I counted five breaths in, five out, and it didn't help.

Along with my thoughts was self-inflicted torture. My mind raced. Had they found Lucy alive, she would be here. They would be thrilled to share that good news with me. Their silence told me what I didn't want to know. Eventually, someone would come and they would say the thing, and then the world would end properly, with a form to sign.

The detectives on true crime shows always said telling a parent their child is dead was the worst part of the job. I could picture a detective dreading doing just that as he or she made their way to my room this very moment.

The jacket. Lucy's jacket. Where was it? I pulled my right hand free of the blanket and found the call button because I could not stop myself. Erin came in rushing in.

"My daughter's jacket," I blurted. She looked at me befuddled. "I had it in my bag, could you bring it to me?" I could feel the warm tears on my cheeks.

Erin looked at me with a sad expression. "I'm sorry, but the police probably have your belongings. Let me check on that for you," she said, bolting out of the room like it was too painful to watch me wallow.

A few minutes later, a uniform peeked through the privacy blanket. Like Erin, he must want to be anywhere else but here with a grieving mother. He took off his hat as he stepped in. He wasn't the one who'd dragged me back from the fire. His hair was too tidy for that.

"Mrs. Morrissey?" he said.

I nodded. My throat swelled on instinct, defending against the answer it thought would come.

"I'm Officer Hudson," he said. "The nurse said you have some questions about—"

"My daughter's jacket," I said, interrupting him.

"Detective Alvarez is en route. He'll help you track your... that down," Hudson said.

"Is she dead?" My voice had found the words again and it tasted like I had drunk soured milk. "Is Lucy dead?"

Hudson's posture changed by half a degree, a thing I would've missed if everything in me wasn't tuned to the frequency of that question. "I don't have confirmed information to release," he said. "Fire is still active at the scene. They're—"

"Is that what you say when you know and you can't tell me," I said, "or when you don't know and you've been trained to sound like you do?" The words surprised us both. They had edges. "Don't do this to me."

He looked, briefly, like a person and not a uniform. "I am sorry." Then the uniform covered him again. "The detective will be here very soon. Do you need anything from me right now?"

"Bring me my daughter," I said.

He looked at the floor. "I'll send your nurse back in." He left without turning his back on me and the door settled in his wake with the softest click I'd ever hated.

I found the seam on the blanket and picked at it until the thread came loose. I pulled and pulled and the blanket did not unravel. They make them that way on purpose. Someone had thought about the hands that would need something to destroy.

A doctor came and said words about fractures and lungs and rest. He had a round face and a voice that had learned to be a pillow. "We were lucky," he said, meaning me. "Good thing you weren't closer to the blast. You'll make a full recovery." He spoke as if healing could be a place.

"Will she?" I asked. "Will Lucy?"

He steadied, then pivoted. "I'm not connected to those updates. I'm sorry."

They were all sorry. The word was a puddle on the floor that reflected nothing.

The doctor left orders and a signature, and a note for physical therapy.

Erin returned with pills in a tiny cup and another cup with a swallow of water. "This will help with the shoulder pain," she said, and held the cup until I took it, as if feeding a baby bird. I placed the pill on my tongue and swallowed, and felt immediately guilty for accepting anything the world offered.

Time moved. I only knew because the second hand of the clock kept yanking forward and because the light over my door blinked twice and then stopped. Noise seeped in under the door: carts rolling, someone laughing, a baby crying far away, the low murmur of a TV with its volume set wrong. My body grew heavier around the edges, a shore eroding under something small and relentless.

THE DOOR BANGED OPEN.

Braden stumbled in at a run, hair wild, chest heaving as if he'd tried to outpace the news. He looked wrong in the light: skin ash-gray, eyes rimmed in red, a smear of soot under one cheekbone. For a second I saw him as he'd been when we first met. In our twenties. Then he was here and older, and as wrecked as I'd ever seen him.

He stopped short at the edge of the bed like there was an invisible fence. "Oh God," he said. "Jenna."

I reached for him with the arm that wasn't tied to me. The movement tugged the sling and my rib complained, but he was already moving, already folding down and around me with the kind of care that would've made me angry if everything didn't hurt. He smelled like smoke, so I knew he had been at the burned-down cabin. His shirt was damp where he'd sweated through it. I pressed my face into the familiar, stupid cotton of his collar and cried.

He cried too. Not the dramatic kind of tears, not the kind that demands attention. The quiet, helpless version that leaks out because the body refuses to keep it in. His shoulders shook. He tried to swallow his grief and couldn't. It made me love him and hate the world for making me remember love.

"I thought—" he started, then shook his head, words failing him. "When I saw— They said—" He pulled back enough to look at me, eyes searching my face like he might find a better outcome there. "You're okay. You're okay."

"I'm not. Lucy." I held his gaze because if I looked away the room would tilt and I would slide off the bed and fall forever. "Do you know anything? Did they tell you anything?"

He sat on the edge of the bed, careful not to jostle the sling and tubes, his hand closing around mine like a promise he couldn't keep. "They're being tight-lipped," he said. "I was at the cabin, but it was still on fire, so they kicked me out. I called everyone I can think of. The station said the scene was active, the fire department said they're coordinating. The word 'coordinating' should be a crime." He swallowed. His Adam's apple moved. "No one will say if—" He glanced down at our hands, our knuckles gone white. "I don't know."

"What about Heather? Did they find her?"

The mention of her name pained him. Not just for what she'd done to him, to our daughter. I could tell the hurt of my not telling him I had a child when I was a teenager hurt him deeply, but he was sparing me from that conversation for now. With everything that was going on, he was showing me mercy. For now.

"They haven't found her either," he said after a moment. "She might have been inside the cabin when it exploded."

I reached for fury—at him for not being the one person on earth with an answer. I thought the Morrisseys could get anything they wanted from anyone. But apparently not this.

"She was just—" I tried and failed to finish that sentence. "I left her," I said instead.

"You didn't," he said automatically, in reflex and mercy. "You were—"

"I left her." I wasn't sure who I meant. Heather, the

daughter I'd left as a newborn or Lucy, the daughter I'd left for Heather to take from me as punishment.

The beeping from my monitor ticked faster, a tattletale.

"You couldn't have known," he said. "Jenna, you couldn't have—"

"She's my daughter." I said it like a verdict. "My job is to know."

He closed his eyes and nodded, not as agreement. As a witness.

We lay there together in the hospital bed without saying anything. Because it hurt too much.

THIRTY-EIGHT

EVEN AT NIGHT, THE HOSPITAL WAS NEVER DARK OR quiet. Not that it mattered; I wouldn't have been able to sleep without knowing where my Lucy was.

"I shouldn't be here," I told Braden, who sat beside my bed, elbows on his knees, head bowed between his hands. He looked up at me, eyes red from exhaustion and tears.

"I should be out there, looking for her."

He sat up and slipped his warm hand into my cold, clammy one. It felt good. He squeezed gently.

"We need to let the professionals handle this now, sweetheart."

Braden didn't mean only the law enforcement officers. He'd doubled the retainer for Emily Acosta, our attorney, unleashing her investigators to find Lucy and Heather. Between the police and Emily's team, he believed they'd be found. I wasn't as confident. Or maybe I just didn't want to know what would be discovered.

When the door opened, I expected another nurse, but it was Detective Alvarez. He was still in the same smoke-stained clothes as when he'd taken my statement earlier, his expression caught somewhere between exhaustion and something heavier.

He shut the door gently and came closer. "Mr. and Mrs. Morrissey." His voice was low, careful. "I wanted to update you before the night shift turns over."

I gripped the blanket so hard the fabric bunched beneath my fingers. "Did they—" I stopped. My throat refused to finish the question.

He drew a slow breath. "They recovered one body from the debris."

Braden straightened, his chair scraping the tile. "One?"

"Is it..." I couldn't finish.

Alvarez gave the universal sign of uncertainty—a short shrug, a quick dip of his head. "I'm sorry, but I don't have a definitive answer right now. The remains were too badly burned to identify visually. Forensics will run DNA, but that'll take time."

The world narrowed to that word—*body*. It had a weight heavier than anything I'd ever heard.

"You think it's Lucy?" The question left a bitter taste in my mouth, made me want to vomit, but I swallowed it back.

The detective hesitated, then said, "We're not jumping to conclusions. Until the lab confirms it, we can't say who it was."

"Not jumping to conclusions," Braden repeated as if he needed to taste the words to understand them. "Surely you can tell if it was a child-sized body?"

Alvarez didn't answer. That silence was worse than the truth.

He cleared his throat. "There's something else."

I looked up; somehow there was still room for more bad news.

"We can't locate Heather," he said. "The vehicle she'd been using was destroyed in the fire, but we've got no indication she was inside, and since there was only one body recovered so far, we've issued an APB in California and Nevada. The FBI and US Marshals are getting involved. If she got out, she won't get far."

My pulse stuttered. "You think she set the fire?"

"We're treating it as arson until proven otherwise," he said carefully. "She's dangerous and desperate. But we'll find her."

"So she could be out there right now."

He nodded once. "That's why I wanted you both to hear this directly from me. We have officers canvassing, and we're pulling surveillance from nearby highways."

The room began spinning again. The same nauseating slow spin I'd felt when the blast threw me to the ground.

One body.

Heather was missing.

The detective skirted around our questions on whether the body found was that of a ten-year-old child, or an adult.

But if the police believed Heather had escaped, and they were out there looking for her, then that meant the body in the cabin was... I stopped myself, but I knew that kind of math would never end right.

Alvarez studied us for another beat. "I'll be in touch the moment we know more." He looked at me, his eyes softening. "Try to rest, Mrs. Morrissey."

"Rest," I repeated. "Right."

He gave a small nod to Braden and left, the door closing with a muted click that sounded too final.

THE QUIET THAT followed wasn't peaceful. It was the kind that hurt inside your ears.

I leaned back against the pillow and stared at the ceiling until the white tiles blurred together. Braden moved his chair closer and took my hand. His grip was firm, but his skin was now as cold as mine.

"They'll find her," he said, tired and trying to sound certain.

I didn't answer. I couldn't stop replaying the detective's words. *One body recovered. Heather can't be found.* It looped like a cruel lullaby.

Outside the window, a pale orange haze hovered over the distant ridge—smoke or dawn, I couldn't tell.

We kept the television off, since our lives had become chum for the frenzied media to feast on.

The oxygen hissed softly at my nose. Every intake of breath hurt my rib, but the pain was something to hold on to. Punishment for what I had unleashed on my family all those years ago.

Braden's head drooped, his hand still wrapped around mine. He'd been awake nearly twenty-four hours. I should've told him to get some sleep at our cabin, but I needed the weight of him there. I watched the line of his shoulders rise and fall with shallow breaths until he drifted into a restless half-sleep.

I didn't sleep. The sedative from earlier had faded, leaving my mind raw. Images from the explosion flickered behind my eyelids each time I blinked; the flare of light, the roar, the heat licking my face. A vision of Lucy—then nothing.

The monitor beeped steadily beside me, a mechanical heart pretending to care.

Somewhere down the hall, a phone rang and stopped.

The smell of antiseptic mixed with the ghost of smoke that still clung to my hair.

Hours stretched and folded over themselves. When I finally looked at the clock again, it was a little after three.

The door opened softly. I expected another nurse with

a vitals check, but the footsteps were heavier. Braden stirred but didn't wake fully.

Then I saw him. Detective Alvarez was standing in the doorway again. I wasn't expecting to see him at three a.m. His presence gave me chills, as if I had an audience with the Grim Reaper. But his face was different this time. For the first time since I'd met him, he was smiling.

I looked down, and beside him, half-hidden behind his arm, was Lucy.

For a moment, I didn't understand what I was seeing. My brain—stubborn from trauma, sedatives, and exhaustion—refused to connect the image to reality. My mind had played that cruel hoax on me too many times to count since Lucy was taken. So I assumed I was once again seeing what I wanted to see when it was just a figment from my head. I blinked and yet there she stood. Could this be real? She looked smaller somehow, wrapped in a gray paramedic blanket, her face smudged with soot, bits of wood and leaves tangled in her hair, eyes wide and blinking against the light.

"Mom," she said, tentative, as if unsure she was allowed to speak.

The world broke open.

I threw back the blanket and tried to stand. Pain exploded through my side, but it didn't matter. I got out of bed, but I was held back by an IV tube, which I yanked free without caring about the consequences. Braden was already up, stumbling to my side as Lucy ran forward. The impact of her body against mine drove a gasp from my lungs. I held her anyway, ignoring every warning about the intense pain I was feeling from my ribs and shoulder. The IV machine beeped angrily.

Even though I was embracing her, part of me still feared this was some sort of drug-induced hallucination. A body had been found, and the detective said they were looking for Heather, so it seemed clear he was telling us that Lucy was dead without saying it. Yet, here she was. Was I dreaming? But I could feel her heartbeat hammering against mine—alive and solid and real.

"Oh my God," I whispered into her messy hair. "Lucy —how—"

Braden wrapped his arms around us both. His tears hit my neck, hot and fast. "You're okay," he kept saying. "You're okay."

Alvarez hovered near the doorway, allowing for the family reunion to unfold unfettered and letting the chaos of relief run its course. When I finally looked up, he gave a faint, tired smile. "We found her about an hour ago," he said. "One of the fire crews saw movement near the tree line. She was hiding out there."

I pulled back enough to look at Lucy. "You were in the woods?"

She nodded, eyes huge. "I thought they were going to find me," she whispered.

"They?" I asked.

"My sister or the fire," she said simply. *My sister.* That took me aback. I felt shame for my lies, for not letting Lucy know she had an older sister. But that was a conversation we needed to have later.

Braden pulled a chair close and guided her onto his lap. She clung to his shirt, still shaking. I sat back on the bed, every nerve screaming but my heart steady for the first time in hours.

Two nurses adjusted the machines but kept their distance, letting me have the moment.

Alvarez stepped closer. "She's okay, all things considered. Scrapes, a little dehydration, but nothing serious. She's been checked by EMTs already."

I pressed a hand over my mouth. Relief hurts as much as pain. "How did you get out?"

Lucy hesitated, glancing from her father to me. "I was locked in a room upstairs. I think it was like an attic. I smelled smoke. There was a little half-moon window. It only opened halfway. I thought I'd get stuck, but I turned sideways and pushed until I could fit. I scraped my arm." She showed the bandage on her forearms and near her elbows. Tears stung my eyes as she continued to tell us about her escape. "Once I squeezed out of there, I slid down the roof and landed on the ground. It hurt, but I was able to get up. I thought I heard you calling my name, so I tried to run to you, but everything went boom. So I ran as fast as I could away from that place and hid."

Braden brushed her hair back, removing a few twigs and flicking them onto the floor, his voice breaking. "Smart girl."

Alvarez added, "If she'd waited even a minute longer..." He didn't finish. He didn't have to.

I reached out and cupped Lucy's face in my hands. "You're safe now." The words felt fragile but true.

Alvarez checked his watch. "I'll let you rest. We'll have more questions later, but tonight—just be together." He started toward the door, then turned back. "We'll keep an officer outside your room until Heather's located. But"—he looked at Lucy—"that was probably who we found inside the cabin." He clearly did not want to get into details in front of her.

"Thank you," I managed.

He nodded and slipped out, closing the door behind him.

A doctor and nurse came in to check Lucy and me. The nurse reattached my IV line, and the doctor ordered scans and X-rays for Lucy just to be safe. While he arranged a room in the children's wing, he left us alone for now.

Lucy fell asleep almost immediately, curled against my side on the narrow hospital bed. Her breathing evened until it was soft and shallow. Braden sat in the chair again, watching her like she might vanish if he blinked.

The room was dim except for the monitors' glow and that soft light that was always on. I could still smell the smoke in her hair. I wanted to wash it out—wash everything out—but I also wanted to keep her exactly like this: real, warm, alive.

Braden reached over and touched my hand.

"We got her back," I whispered.

"Heather didn't win," he said.

I nodded, somber. Outside the window, the horizon was paling. The faintest hint of dawn pushed against the dark. I exhaled shakily, letting the night drain out of me.

Alvarez's earlier words crept back into my head, threading through the quiet like smoke.

One body recovered. APBs on Heather.

If Lucy was here... then that meant...

I glanced at Braden, then down at our sleeping daughter.

"So that must have been Heather's body they found," I whispered.

I felt a wave of sadness wash over me then guilt for feeling sad about her death. I couldn't admit this to Braden, but much as I wanted to hate Heather, much as I wanted to feel nothing about her dying in that explosion, I couldn't. She was—after everything she'd put us through—

my daughter too. I had just lost my first born daughter. Was I not allowed to grieve for her?

THIRTY-NINE

THREE WEEKS HAD PASSED SINCE THE EXPLOSION, BUT sometimes, in the middle of the night, I still woke to the echo of it; the flash, the pressure, the roar that turned the world white. I could still feel the searing heat on my face.

I made my way down the stairs. The only sounds were the coffee machine in the kitchen and Sunny's pitter-patter on the tile, his nose up to check if I'd brought anything worth sharing. "Sorry, boy—nothing good right now." The smell of coffee filled the air—ordinary scents that still felt like small miracles. For the first time since Heather entered our lives, the house felt like home again. It helped that my shoulder and ribs were healing; the place no longer felt like a hospital.

A couple hours later, Emily arrived for a debrief. I poured her a cup of coffee. Emily, Braden, and I sat around the kitchen island. I could feel my heart racing and it wasn't from the caffeine.

She pulled out an iPad Pro from her luxury leather tote bag and opened it. Putting on her stylish reading glasses low on her nose.

"Tell me what you know," I said.

Emily tapped her screen. "Unofficially, the working theory is that Heather tampered with the propane tank. The forensics team found evidence the main line was opened manually. Five hundred gallons of liquefied propane gas leaked out. That's what caused the explosion once the vapor built up."

"So it was deliberate."

"It sure looks that way," Emily said. "She knew what she was doing. Once she let the propane out, the cops believe she set a small fire, they think in a garbage bin."

I stared down at the black coffee swirling in my cup. "So she blew herself up thinking Lucy was still locked in that room upstairs. On purpose."

Emily's tone softened. "That's what the police think. The remains were female, five-foot-five, same height as Heather. The right age range. The preliminary bone analysis fits her all the way."

"But they won't say it was her," I said, frustrated.

She hesitated. "Not yet. DNA's a mess. They said months, maybe longer, before a definitive match. But the body was almost completely incinerated, so we might never get that DNA match. Still, between the height, the structure, the location... Well, if it walks like a duck, Jenna..."

I rubbed at my shoulder, the one that still throbbed from the blast. "And the motive?"

"She had a long, violent history," Emily said. "Criminal record, mental-health issues. In her mind, this was probably the ultimate revenge—go out in flames, take you down emotionally without going back to prison. The detectives are calling it a murder-suicide attempt. But Lucy was able to escape."

My stomach turned. Had Lucy not managed to get out of there in time, it wouldn't have been an attempt. She hated me that much that she was willing to end her life, and Lucy's. Losing both my daughters in one horrific violent act. It made my skin crawl.

"Thank God, Lucy got out on time," I said. Braden put his hand over mine.

"She's a remarkable, quick-thinking kid. Had she not squeezed out of that tiny window—" Emily said.

"Let's not even go there," I interrupted, dabbing the corner of my eyes.

Emily hesitated, scrolling through her notes again. "There's one more thing," she said. "You'll want to hear this."

I braced myself. "What now?"

"Turns out Heather, well, *Ashley*, wasn't just running

cons on you and Braden. The Feds think she embezzled over two million dollars from the law firm's escrow accounts. And she was also behind a hacker crew that the feds suspect stole tens of thousands of Bitcoin from a cryptocurrency exchange."

"Jesus," Braden muttered.

"She told me this wasn't about money when I offered to pay a large ransom for Lucy's release."

Emily gave a humorless laugh. "No. She was already loaded. She didn't need the money. It was personal. She wanted to hurt you."

I nodded slowly as I soaked up all this dastardly information.

And now, I finally understood what she'd meant by saying this wasn't about money. It was to hurt me by destroying my life with Braden, but when that didn't work, she found another way to really hurt me by trying to kill Lucy.

Still. Something seemed off.

"Lucy keeps saying she heard two women yelling before the explosion."

Emily looked up. "Yeah, I saw that in the report. The detectives noted it, but they don't think it means much. She was half-conscious, heavily sedated most of the time. It could have been a hallucination from the drugs or the television or even Heather ranting and raving to herself. Some sort of psychotic break."

"Maybe." Yet Lucy wasn't one to invent stories. She'd whispered it that first night in the hospital—*two women yelling*—and it still looped in my mind like a skipped record.

"Well, let law enforcement figure that out. Whatever happened up there, it's over for you guys," Emily said looking at me and Braden with a smile.

Over. The word sounded too final. I wasn't sure I believed in endings anymore.

Emily's investigator uncovered why Heather ended up in foster care when I'd been told she was adopted at birth by a loving couple. It hadn't been a lie. On that awful day they took my baby, she was handed to her new parents—Ed and Shirley Halloway. They were exactly what the agency promised: kind people who couldn't have children and had been waiting for years to adopt a child. While my world was splitting open, theirs was beginning.

Three years later a drunk driver destroyed all of it.

The police report said the Halloways died at the scene. Ashley—my daughter's name then—was strapped into a car seat in the back. She survived. "Miraculously," the notes said, as if the word could hold the weight of what came next: months of treatment and physical therapy, some head trauma. The file didn't talk about prognosis; it moved her, briskly, to "placement."

Emily wondered, gently, whether the injury might have left a shadow—mood swings, depression, impaired judgment—symptoms sometimes seen with chronic traumatic encephalopathy. Maybe. CTE can't be confirmed without examining brain tissue after death, so we would probably never know.

I told myself I wasn't looking for excuses. I told myself I only wanted a reason—something other than "she's evil," the way my father would have stamped it and been done. I held on to the thought that a collision and that head injury had tilted her life off its line—that harm has a lineage. If the Halloways hadn't died, maybe none of this would have happened. It didn't absolve her. It didn't absolve me. But it kept the world from being as simple and cruel as my father always said it was.

Recovery from my injuries from the explosion was slower than I wanted but eventually, I turned a corner. Physical therapy for my shoulder, and mental therapy for the three of us. Braden never missed an appointment. Neither did Lucy. She liked to sit in the waiting room sketching trees—always the same ones, tall with twisting branches that reached toward each other but never touched.

Braden and I went to therapy every Tuesday. Braden joked that if we survived therapy in Marin County, we could survive anything.

One afternoon, after a session, he lingered in the car before starting the engine. "You know," he said, "I'm not angry about what you did back then. About giving her up. I can't even imagine what you had to go through."

I turned to him. "Then what are you angry about?"

"That you didn't trust me enough to tell me." His eyes were tired but kind. "You were a kid, Jenna. You had asshole parents. You did the best you could."

"I wanted to tell you right when we first met," I said through a tight throat, "but I had been brainwashed into thinking I had done something wrong. That I was evil. Still, you're so right. I should have told you. A long, long time ago."

He smiled faintly. "That's in the past now. Let's just try to be honest moving forward."

I smiled. "I like that."

He started the car but didn't pull out of the lot. "The firm called again," he said. "Apologized for how they handled things."

"Are you going back?" I asked. He shrugged, staring through the windshield. "I don't know. Maybe I'm done having my future in anyone's hands but mine. I've been killing myself for a firm that kicked me to the curb without as much of an internal investigation. Maybe I hang out my own shingle. Pick my cases. Spend more time with you and Lucy."

I smiled. "That sounds good."

"It sounds...possible," he said, and for the first time in

months, I saw a trace of the man I'd married—not the lawyer, not the provider, but the partner.

And I liked that idea very much.

A couple weeks later, I felt good enough to once again meet up with Madison for our usual brunch. She had asked to brunch on several occasions, but I didn't feel ready, even after my shoulder, and ribs had healed. It was a sense of skittishness after everything Heather put me through, but I was also embarrassed about the Marin mom's pointing and whispering about me. But finally, I began to regain my confidence, and thanks to therapy, accepted that I had done nothing wrong, and I had nothing to be ashamed of about my past.

Madison hugged me tightly. "You're the talk of Marin," she whispered against my hair.

"Let them talk," I said, and smiled into my mimosa.

Madison laughed, but her eyes darted, measuring me, checking for cracks. I allowed her to see none. Sitting there among the gossip and clinking glasses felt like a quiet rebellion—proof that I could exist in sunlight again, even if every glare of a camera phone made me flinch inside.

When I got home that afternoon, Braden and Lucy were on the back deck. He was helping her with homework, though it looked more like drawing than math. She waved when she saw me, the motion quick and birdlike.

"Mom! Look!"

She held up a sketchbook. Two trees, their branches almost touching.

"Beautiful," I said, and meant it.

She grinned. "Dad says we should go hiking this weekend."

"Sounds perfect."

Her grin faded a little. "I had that dream again," she said quietly. "The one about the fire."

Braden's hand brushed her hair. "It's okay, chickadee."

She looked at me. "There were two women yelling."

The same words, the same eerie calm. My chest tightened.

"I know, sweetheart," I said. "I believe you. But it's all over now."

She nodded but didn't look convinced.

After she went inside, Braden wrapped his arms around me gently. "She'll heal."

"I know," I said, though the back of my neck prickled.

THAT NIGHT, after everyone was asleep, I sat at the kitchen table again. I couldn't sleep.

On my phone, I scrolled through the latest update from Emily: *DNA inconclusive. Further testing pending.*

I set the phone face down. It had to be her.

Outside, the wind stirred the trees. The same kind of

night as the one up in Tahoe—cold, still, waiting for something to ignite.

Despite everything Heather had done, I couldn't make myself feel glad she was dead. Pity wasn't the right word either. It was heavier than that, deeper—like mourning the version of yourself you never became.

I looked toward Lucy's room, where the night light glowed faintly beneath the door.

No mother should have to lose a daughter.

Even one like Heather, who did such horrible things.

EPILOGUE

ONE YEAR LATER

I heard Lucy before I saw her; the infectious laughter of a child in the wind, a ribbon of sound that tugged along the backyard and up through the open kitchen window. Braden whooped a second later and the two of them pranced outside with Sunny chasing after them, two silhouettes against a sky the color of clean porcelain. A giant red and yellow Seahorse kite wobbled and danced above our little strip of Marin.

Inside, the house smelled like honey, soy, and lime as charcoal wafted in from outside. I'd already marinated the chicken for the Mother's Day grilling, sliced strawberries for shortcake, and set out the stack of paper plates I swore I wouldn't use this year and then did anyway for the sake of convenience.

Lana Del Rey's dreamy voice bellowed from the Echo

Show device on the shelf with her haunting version of Sublime's "Doin' Time."

The mail was a thick lopsided stack the carrier had somehow wedged through the slot. One glance and I knew most of it was headed for the recycling bin. For a state chasing a Zero Waste plan, you'd think they'd start with prohibiting junk mail. Yet I diligently sorted it on the island: a dental reminder, a glossy catalog full of dresses meant for women who never sit, several credit offers with too many exclamation marks.

Near the bottom, an envelope waited, cream-colored and just heavy enough to feel important. I could tell by its shape and the weight of the stock that it was a greeting card. Mother's Day, I assumed, so I plucked it from the stack.

The envelope was adorned with glittery paper roses. For a moment I was confused. Braden and Lucy had already given me their cards this morning. Who sent me this one?

Then something cold slid through me. I knew. I'd felt it the moment I touched the envelope, a pull I didn't want to acknowledge.

I examined the card. No return address. Then I saw the La Poste stamp—France. My stomach dropped. I knew exactly who had sent it, even without a name.

I opened it with shaking hands. Scratchy rosettes,

glitter dusting my thumb as I slid a finger under the fold and I gently eased the card out.

More tiny, tacky rosettes made of a scratchy fabric and dusted with a sparse, flaking pink glitter greeted me inside. The front of the card had an an overly sentimental and saccharine message:

✿✿ *Happy Mother's Day to the Best Mom in the Whole Wide World!* ✿✿

I opened the card. Inside, letters that were designed to connect smoothly, mimicking natural cursive handwriting with decorative loops and extended tails, added an extra touch of faux fancy elegance.

From the moment I took my first breath,
you've been my guiding light, my safe place,
and the heart of our family.
Your love is endless, your strength inspiring,
and your kindness touches everyone you meet.
Today and every day, I'm grateful for you—
for your hugs, your laughter,
and all the little things you do that make life
beautiful.
Happy Mother's Day to the woman who does
it all with grace, love, and a smile.

No signature. No personalized scribble. No flourish. A

card bought, not written. A sentiment borrowed and mailed forward, as is.

All the way from France.

I set the card on the island and let my trembling hand rest on it. The paper was smooth in a way that felt deliberate, as if someone had thought about that too. Outside, Lucy shrieked with delight. A fresh gust of wind picked up the kite as it dipped and lifted, tail flicking.

I turned the envelope over. The postmark blurred at the edges, a ring of smudged ink and a date in numbers. The return corner was clean. The sender wished to remain anonymous, but I knew who had sent it, and my entire body tensed up. She might not have signed it, but by sending this over-the-top flowery card to me, she had.

Braden leaned in the doorway, his windswept hair pushed back, cheeks pinked from the sun. "You coming out? We're about to try the double-handle trick."

"Give me one minute," I said. He must have picked up by looking at me that something was off.

He walked over, peered at the card, and gave a low whistle. "Whoa. Someone found the most cringey one to send to you, huh?" He squinted, looking at it. "Wait. Who sent you—"

I kept my voice soft. "There's no name on it."

Braden looked up. I could tell he, too, knew who'd sent the unsigned card. Heather.

We stared at each other in stunned silence. He reached for my hand and held it tightly. I squeezed back.

Lucy yelled, "Dad!" from the yard. The Seahorse tugged above like it was alive.

"Go," I said. "I'll be right there."

He squeezed my fingers and went back outside. I stood in the kitchen for a moment, staring out the window and watching my family.

I picked up the card again, and this time it felt razor sharp against my fingers. The words inside were anyone's, and that was the point. She'd chosen a voice that belonged to everyone and no one with the sappiest message a greeting card writer could regurgitate, knowing she meant none of it.

The authorities seemed convinced that Heather had died in the cabin explosion she'd set, although the identity of the body recovered had still not been positively identified. They were so sure that they were no longer actively looking for her.

Until I received some sort of forensic DNA proof, I wasn't so sure. I could still feel her in my gut. Like she was out there. Plotting her next move to destroy me, and my family.

It *wasn't about money,* she'd told me. It never was about that.

I held the card close to my nose as if I could smell some faint clue as to where she was, because I doubted she was actually in France. Of course it smelled of just thick card-stock and fading ink.

Setting it down, I traced the tiny cardstock flowers with my finger, then slid it back into the envelope and pressed the flap shut like that made any difference. I rubbed the back of my hands so they would stop trembling. The room was bright and ordinary. Lana Del Rey carried on as if this were an ordinary Mother's Day.

Outside, Lucy shouted again, a bright burst of sound. "Mom! Come on!" Sunny joined in with a playful bark.

"I'm coming," I called.

I should have called the police. Instead, I tucked the card at the bottom of our everything drawer and walked out into the sun.

Costa Brava, Spain

I LIKED IT OUT HERE. The sea didn't pretend. It didn't care what you said you were, what you'd done in the past, or what you wished; it took the shape of the wind and the bottom beneath it, and then it went on being what it had always been for millions of years. It was comforting to feel so tiny.

The luxurious motor yacht swayed as lightly as breath on the Mediterranean. The afternoon was an advertisement for the tourism board, with water so blue it bordered on parody. Whitecaps like knuckles, a sky with no plans. The captain had anchored far enough from shore that the world went silent. There were no vendors, no sunburned tourists in too-tight speedos, no children whining about sand in their shoes, no lovers getting frisky on oversized beach towels. Out here it was just gulls, blue water, and the soft, domestic clink of glass.

I lay back, topless—when in Rome—on a towel that cost more than the clothes I used to own in a year, watching the shadow of my wide-brimmed hat slide across my thighs. The sangria sweated in my hand, drops sliding down the glass like they were late to something. I lifted it and let the ice kiss my lip.

It wasn't the first time I had reinvented myself, and I was certain it wouldn't be the last time either. People think a new life feels like a fresh start. It doesn't, because whatever shit you bring along in your head from your past lives on. It follows you to the new one. If only one of those *Men in Black* neuralyzers were real—wipe the bad memories with a flash of light. But even if it existed, I'm not sure I'd use it. The things I survived didn't just scar me; they built me. Sharpened me.

Made me fearless.

A year was enough to get comfortable with my new name—the one on the fake passport. I became the socialite I'd invented. Daughter of a tech billionaire. The bank smiled at the numbers I deposited with them, and staff at the luxury hotels and villas I had visited always moved before I asked, treating me like royalty, convinced people with this face and these bank accounts are always handed things.

It was not enough to forget the look someone I did, on some level, care for gave me when I raised a gun and truth arrived.

I didn't plan to run after Monalisa that night. I meant to let the door finish its creaking and settle, the night sit like a lid, the house thrum with the noise of a rattling furnace. But I heard the truck door, the choked sound her throat made, and the part of me that doesn't tolerate leaving stood up.

"Monalisa," I called, running after her. "Wait." And even then I might have meant it, the reach of that word, the cheap grace of it.

She opened the truck's door and turned. The porch light cut her in half, one side candle, one side stone. Her mouth made a circle, a child surprised by her own breath. When I stepped off the porch, gravel shifted and the sound traveled up the dark like a secret.

"Don't go." My voice had the right break in it. I'm good at that.

She smiled in a cracked way that made me feel a little guilt. Relief can be blinding; like an animal walking up towards a butcher to be petted. The smile broke just as the gun came level. I figured she would lunge at me. She was always a fighter, yet she stood there, defeated. Broken-hearted, I suppose. Acceptance is a face I know. It's what you get when someone has already been told everything that matters about themselves and found no argument that sticks.

"I always have your back," she'd been telling me since we were teenagers, so maybe the way she stood there still apparently accepting what I was about to do was her saying it one more time without uttering a word.

I pulled the trigger.

The report was smaller than that night years ago when I shot my foster father—more snap than roar, a sound that didn't echo so much as bite.

A loud, sharp crack that was muffled by the trees. She folded as if a hinge had let go.

It wasn't personal. People say that to make themselves feel bigger than they are, but sometimes it's true. It was arithmetic. The kind with no forgiveness baked in. I would always choose myself over anyone else. Monalisa should have known that, since she was the one who had engrained it into my head over the years.

I had once again pivoted. Liquefied propane is patient until it isn't. I opened the valves on the tank and lit the fumes.

As I worked on the tank, I thought about rain. About how water can give life, and take it. Monalisa told me I was obsessed with my birth mother. I thought it was the usual self-help bullshit she liked to gleam off all those books she read. But at that moment, I knew she was right. I could have disappeared with her into the sunset, yet I chose to end it with a literal bang.

Let Jenna live knowing the daughter she had abandoned had taken the life of the daughter she hadn't. Never to see either of us again.

But then that damned attic window.

I noticed it when I locked her in the room. I checked it out and figured there was no way that spoiled brat would have the survival instinct to try to escape through it. Even if she did manage to do it, the drop to the ground was long. I was wrong. I should have nailed it shut, but hindsight and all that.

People always said that Monalisa and I looked alike. How if you looked at us side by side from the right angle, we were the same person. Height. Weight. Our skin complexion was different, but that didn't matter when burnt bones were all that was left. I figured even if they did identify her eventually, I would be long gone.

She'd always had my back. She had it now too, in death. I'm not sentimental about it. I'm grateful.

The crew's laugh drifted from the flybridge, low and nothing to do with me. They walked on eggshells around me, and I liked it.

I sank back into the chaise lounge. I looked from

behind my Christian Dior chunky square sunglasses at the shadows of gulls stitched into the surface of the water; their harsh, piercing cry cut through the steady sound of the waves. I took another drink of sangria, the orange slice sinking under ice.

There was no need to send the card. I shouldn't have. But I wanted to.

Most kids I'd met in foster care wondered more about their birth mothers than their fathers. Maybe because with a mother you're sure of one thing: She was there. A father might be a question mark. And once you learned what a body endures to deliver a child, walking away felt impossible to square.

Even before I knew my father was killed in Afghanistan by the time I was two, my thoughts kept circling back to my mother. The wondering didn't stay soft. It hardened into bitterness. Then rage.

Sure, my adopted parents were supposed to be good people, but they died when I was three, and I don't remember them. They didn't shape me. The foster care system did. And she did. My birth mother. From the moment she handed me off to be someone else's problem.

I used to think about her on Mother's Day, back when I was a kid, before I even knew her name or that she was even alive. And I still did, after everything that had gone down.

Mother's Day has always seemed silly if you look at it

too closely. A made-up holiday to sell cards and overpriced flowers. A day to celebrate a woman for doing what billions have done throughout time—give birth.

I'd bought the card before I left the States and kept it with me the whole time. I drove up the coast to a small village in the south of France and slid it into a yellow La Poste box, properly stamped, no name and no return. If the mail ran on time, it would land on Mother's Day.

Ordinary is the best disguise—it wears everyone's face.

When I pictured the moment the envelope found her hands, I smiled. What would she feel? Fear? Relief? What would she do—clutch the daughter she loves? Dial 911? Call Interpol? Or just shove it in a drawer and pretend it never existed?

A gull that had been circling settled on the rail—noisy a moment ago, quiet now, its hard eyes regarding me with suspicion. It looked just like the gulls I would see in the San Francisco Bay. I smirked. "Visiting from Vista Bay?"

I raised my glass and took a long, slow sip.

Sometimes I let myself think about the little one. I still couldn't think of her as my half sister, although I know she was. I had misjudged her, and I don't misjudge often. She carried a streak I recognized: a thread of iron stitched into sweetness.

The half-moon window had been tiny, with a twenty-foot drop, and yet she'd stepped through it and jumped to freedom. I respected that. It didn't fit the plan, but she had earned her reward: life.

I've read before, in books I can't remember, that life wants meaning. Life wants what it can get. It wanted me, and I let it.

Again I thought of Monalisa's last look, the way it had held no surprise. We'd both grown up learning the answers to tests no one sane would write. In the end, she recognized the question. I answered.

The captain's voice cut through the memory. "Beautiful spot for a swim over there, ma'am. Want me to head that way?"

I shook my head. "Another sangria."

Leaning back, I let the hat slide lower, the brim cutting the world in half. Far off, a bell on a smaller boat knocked —like a church steeple.

The stewardess brought me my drink. I said nothing as she scurried back to the captain. I wondered if they were getting it on.

I lifted my glass and watched a bead of condensation race to my wrist bone. The sea breathed under us, steady and indifferent.

I smiled.

Life was good.

ABOUT THE AUTHOR

Alan Petersen was born in Costa Rica and now lives in San Francisco, California with his wife and their bossy Chihuahua.

He writes psychological and crime thrillers and hosts the long-running podcast *Meet the Thriller Author*, where he interviews bestselling writers like Dean Koontz, Walter Mosley, Freida McFadden, and Lee Child.

When he's not writing or podcasting, he's watching creepy movies, diving into true-crime docs, or roaming San Francisco's steep hills plotting his next twisty story.

Learn more at AlanPetersen.com.

ALSO BY ALAN PETERSEN

Standalone Psychological Thrillers

The Basement

Imposter Syndrome

The Casual Date

The Elijah Shaw-Alexandra Needham Crime Thriller Series

Gringo Gulch

The Past Never Dies

Always There

Under A Crimson Moon

The Pete Maddox Thriller Series

The Asset

She's Gone

Odd Jobs